Oh, Those Harper Girls!

OH, THOSE HARPER GIRLS!

OR Young and Dangerous

BY KATHLEEN KARR

Author of ☞ It Ain't Always Easy

FARRAR, STRAUS AND GIROUX   NEW YORK

For Pam and Melanie,
gone to Texas

OH, THOSE HARPER GIRLS!

Dear Gentle Reader,

Daddy started us off early in a life of crime. It must have had something to do with his frustration in siring six daughters. We came mostly with the spring, one after the other, barely a year 'twixt each of us: March, April, May, June, July; and then there was me, Lily. I came in April, too, but they'd already used up that month. I guess I've always been the maverick of the family. So it's only natural I should be telling this story of the infamous Harper Girls. It's all Gospel truth, right on up to the part about jail, our brief stage career, and everything. I tell it now in the belief that it may be an object lesson for one and all. Also, I need the money, so I hope you buy a copy of my little book.

Sincerely,

Lily Harper Hogan

1902

1

☞ It all started in Texas, north and some distance to the west of San Antonio. It was God's country then, and it pretty much still is now. It's the part of Texas that gets heavy hot for half the year, and unexpected cold for the rest. It's the last heave of hills before the flatness and dry heat of the desert badlands beyond.

The War for the Confederacy had been over for a few years, at least the fighting part, and things were depressed. The Harper ranch was spread out over scruffy hills topped with stunted greenery. It went into arroyos and up against rocky bluffs. Through the main canyon at the bottom of all this flowed the Hollering Woman Creek. The creek was named after Mama. Family tradition had it that that's what she did the first day Daddy hauled her out to the place after they were married. She'd been born and bred with a little style in San Antonio, and had expected better things for her life. But she got used to the ranch fast, having no other options, and by the time all six Harper girls had arrived she was a typical backcountry woman: overworked and mostly silent.

Slung up next to the Hollering Woman Creek were the buildings: a low ranch house with a sagging roof, an empty bunkhouse in worse repair, and a sort of winter stable and tack room for such horses and stock as might be available and needing a little shelter come the bad weather. Around all this was built a maze of rickety fencing for corrals. That's what had happened to all the cottonwoods that used to grow along the creek.

By the late spring of 1869, the Double H Ranch (named after Daddy, Hy Harper) had seen better days. A fluke blizzard and the Texas Fever had destroyed most of the herd he'd been building up, and the spring drought was worse than usual. Then there was that letter Daddy had just picked up at Fredericksburg. It was from the bank in San Antonio, talking about something called "foreclosure," if he didn't come up with a certain amount of money to give them before the end of the year. That meant somebody would take away the ranch, and never ever give it back. It didn't seem right, somehow, especially if you figure all the sweat and love he'd put into the place.

The particular day it all started, Daddy, always a skinny, nervous man, stood in the dead center of his domain. He was pulling at the few remaining hairs on his head, trying to figure out how to hang on to his ranch and keep his women fed and, even worse, clothed. He squinted up at the burning orb of sun in the sky, like he was maybe looking for God. Then he shrugged his shoulders and trotted off toward the house.

"Lily!"

"Yes, Daddy?"

"Round up them Frivolous Females. I got a new job of work I'm aiming to break you all into this afternoon."

Lily dropped the bucket of water she was hauling up from the creek and set off at a run for her sisters, wondering what surprises her daddy had in store for them this time. Whatever it was, she hoped the timing on it would be better than that project a while back, when he'd decided to dam up the creek for irrigation, only the creek had barely started filling out when the monsoons struck and the whole thing came busting apart over their lowlands, taking the henhouse and outhouse with it. He'd had to rebuild the outhouse, but the hens had just moved into the bunkhouse, and because there'd been no hired help since Lily could remember, it had been left at that.

Lily found May and Julie in the summer kitchen tacked onto the back of the house. It wasn't hard. All she had to do was follow the excruciating sounds coming from May's throat. May was the musical one, although her talents did seem to lie more with the guitar than with her voice. The two were cleaning up from the midday meal. May interrupted the scales she'd been bellowing out to pat her honey-blond hair with a damp hand and fix a vexatious glance on her youngest sister.

"Lily, where's that water you were fetching?"

"I ain't your servant, May, even though you just turned sixteen. I'm on a mission for Daddy. He wants us all outside. Where's the rest?"

May frowned just like their mama did sometimes, and motioned toward the bedroom wing of the house.

"Mama's helping the others with their summer frocks," Julie said, pouting, "and we got stuck with kitchen duty."

Lily ignored Julie's mood. Being almost fourteen seemed to do strange things to a body. Lately, Julie always did seem to be somewhere between tears and a full sulk—except when she was concentrating on that embroidery of hers. "Don't see what they want summer dresses for, anyways. From season to season, nobody gets off this spread."

"Mama says that has to change," interjected May. "Now that April and March are marrying age." She stopped to trill a little celebratory *la-ti-do*. Lily shuddered.

"Seventeen and eighteen. Just think," May added dreamily, "in another year I'll be of age, too. Just let me off this place once and see if I ever come back!"

Lily interrupted the wishful thinking. "Anybody let Daddy in on this marrying project?"

"Mama talked it over with him last night," Julie said. "June and I heard them through the bedroom wall."

"Maybe that's why he's acting so downhearted today," Lily

responded. "It'll cost him to lose a few of us to husbands."

Lily left for the bedrooms. "Your snood's drooping again, Julie!" she threw back over her shoulder. There wasn't much worry about losing Julie to a husband. She already looked and acted about ninety-five, with that stupid net she insisted on stuffing her bun of hair into.

Lily found her mother and other sisters puzzling over a stack of old dresses. There was rarely money for new cloth, and when there was, March, the oldest, always got to use it for a new dress. After she'd worn it a season or so, it was passed on down the line to April. By the time the dregs got to Lily, there wasn't much left to work with. Being a realist, Lily had avoided the whole issue of hand-me-downs in favor of her father's old britches and boiled shirts. All she had to do was roll up the cuffs and she was in business. It was a sight easier.

Mama was working through the pile, a line of frustration creasing her brow. She'd been pretty once, and still kept her dainty figure, but her blond hair had long since washed into a sandy gray, and her face showed the wear of too many downhill battles. All the girls save Lily took after her looks, blond and delicate, right down to gray-blue eyes and almost identical heart-shaped faces. Lily, already past her mother's height, often wondered from what part of the family tree she'd inherited her thick, glossy, almost black hair, and the round chin and hazel eyes that didn't seem to match anybody else's, not to mention her sturdy, less than delicate frame.

"I just don't know, girls. Your daddy said there wasn't any money for new cloth this year. Not even a bolt of cheap calico like the freedmen use—"

"Wouldn't use nigra cloth anyway, Mama."

"Now, don't you be putting on airs, Miss March. With your daddy about to lose everything he's put his life into, we're not much better off than those poor souls, no matter how you think about it."

March had been kind of mincing around, modeling a fragment of cloth across her shoulders, atop her old blue-flowered gingham dress. Now she stopped in a haughty pose, her eyes flashing. "Mama! Don't you ever call us white trash!"

Mama ignored the posture, answering absentmindedly but matter-of-factly, "Maybe not trash, for I did teach you all to read and sew, and I did my best with manners, too, but poor white just the same. Maybe if we took a different approach to the problem, used a bit of this old yellow silk, a little of that green taffeta—"

"Mama, you know those colors make me look ghastly!"

"It could be like a quilt!" June piped up from where she was lounging across the bed. It seemed to Lily that June had been looking at the optimistic side of things for her entire fifteen years. If she didn't like the color of the sky or the day's climate—always telegraphed by the state of frizz on her own head of thicker yellow hair—she'd just pretend it was otherwise. In this part of Texas, it took a fair piece of pretending.

"Exactly, dear," answered Mama. "A dress of many colors."

"I refuse to step out in patchwork," March grumbled, slinging the cloth from her shoulders back onto the pile in a pique. Lily's oldest sister, who never pretended at anything, knew exactly what she wanted. She always had: something finer and more expensive than whatever she'd been born to on this ranch.

April, a slightly paler and less passionate version of March, spoke up. Her voice was generally high-pitched, breathy, and considerably more tentative than March's. Even her hair was a lanker, more tentative shade of flax. "If you're so disinclined, March, I'll take the new dress. Patchwork is better than holes any way you think about it. Isn't it? And if we add enough colors, it might just improve the cast of my complexion." She glanced in the nearby mirror, then back to Mama. "Mightn't it?"

Lily, standing by, tugging at her one long braid, had heard enough. "Joseph wore a coat of many colors in the Bible, and see where it got him! Besides, I suspect the dressmaking is finished for the day. Daddy is waiting on us all outside. I think he has a new scheme."

When the round of groans had subsided, Lily's sisters trooped out after her, leaving their mama bent over wardrobes of the past.

Daddy led his daughters into the cool shade of the stable, scattering two reclining hens and a duck out of the way. He stopped at the workbench he'd set up along one wall. Reaching high, he pulled down a branding iron. "You all know what this is."

"It's what you've hardly used this spring, Daddy, on account of most of the breeding stock expired over the winter."

"Thank you, Lily." He studied the heavy tool with its three straight vertical lines intersected by a horizontal one. "You ever notice the similarity betwixt our Double H brand and that of Izzy Henry's over to the south of us?"

Lily answered again. Her sisters rarely wasted time on such considerations. "Just half a horizontal bar missing, Daddy. You know that."

"Right. And Izzy's cattle somehow made it better than ours through the winter. Not even a touch of the Fever!" He stared past the girls at a bare spot on the wall behind them, like he couldn't figure it out nohow, then shook his head. "Now, it strikes me that a little sharing of the wealth at this point in time wouldn't be too much of a hardship on Izzy. A kind of silent loan. We'd pay him back, of course, in a year or two, when our herd comes back up to snuff—"

"Rustling!" It was March, putting fiber into her voice like she did when she wanted everybody to know she was the oldest, and therefore undoubtedly the smartest. "You want to turn your daughters into cattle rustlers!"

Daddy smiled. His girls caught on fast when it mattered.

"But they *hang* cattle rustlers, Daddy!" June said.

"It's been known to happen on occasion, daughter. But have no fear. That's the beauty of my plan. Ain't no one ever hung a child rustler, nor a young lady, either. So I figure if I give you instructions, then send you off—"

"By ourselves?" May's voice went up a whole octave till the question was gotten out.

"That'd be the whole point, wouldn't it? By yourselves, but in disguise. Like Lily here wears all the time. You'd seem like any cowhand, unless you got caught, of course. I wouldn't recommend getting caught."

"But it wouldn't be nice, Daddy." Julie was dabbing at her eyes. "It would be *wrong*."

"Wrong!" he burst out. "It isn't wrong the bank in San Antone is fixing to take away everything I got? My entire life's work? Leaving me with a loving wife and six daughters to feed and clothe? It's not wrong that we could be cast out without a penny and nowheres to go? Nowheres at all?"

"Oh!" gasped April.

There was a deathly lull as the six girls considered the possibilities of what Daddy said.

Acceptance was easiest for Lily. She knew exactly how Daddy felt about the ranch, feeling the same way herself. To keep something that meant so much to the two of them, well, she'd go to quite a few lengths. And he had said they'd pay Izzy Henry back. Besides, Lily was rather intrigued by the idea. She turned to her sisters. June and Julie were still dazed, but March, April, and May had their yellow heads bent together. When they broke apart, March was the spokesman, as usual.

"Say we do this thing, even though it goes against everything Mama's taught us all these years. Supposing we make a little exception, just this once . . . What do we get out of it, Daddy?"

"What do you get out of it? Confound it, daughter, you shouldn't be thinking on what you get out of it! Should be thinking on how to help your poor old daddy in his time of tribulation!"

9

"It's not poor old Daddy who might get caught, is it?"

He shifted uncomfortably and rubbed his four-day beard. "Well, what do you want out of it, then?"

"If we find you enough to make a difference, Daddy, to help make the bank payments, we want a trip into San Antonio and new dresses for all of us."

He sighed.

"A long trip, so we get to go to a few dances and meet quality people."

"And an evening at the theater," June quickly added.

Daddy was pulling at his hair again.

"If you don't stop that, Daddy, you won't have a blessed thing left growing atop your head."

"Lay off me, Lily. You'd be bald, too, if you'd sired such a passel of buzzards." He looked at his eldest. "Right, March. After the cattle drive at the end of summer. If there are any to drive. Now, there's no reason to be worrying your mother about any of this . . ." But his flock had already flown.

Being thirteen and the youngest, Lily was usually left to her own resources. The coalitions in the family seemed to form around the three oldest sisters, then the next two in line, June and Julie. While all had been trained into their chores on the ranch, the five oldest performed them only perfunctorily, leaving more time to mope and grumble around the place.

Lily, on the other hand, took to ranching with enthusiasm. She was always interested in how and why something had to be done, rather than just getting the job over with. Thus, her older sisters knew she had a better idea of what might be involved in the new family undertaking than any of them. So she became the ringleader.

The Harper girls were gathered by the creek after supper that night. All but Lily had stripped down to their chemises against the thick heat, cooling their toes in the water. Lily was

10

cooling her toes, too, but she didn't own a chemise to strip down to, so just had her trousers rolled up above her knees, enjoying the swirl of creek water and letting her sisters work things out in their minds.

March now considered the whole undertaking a great challenge. It was, after all, a means to a very desirable end in her eyes: a new wardrobe and access to the high-toned Anglo society of San Antonio. It was she who spoke first.

"All right, Lilykins, how do we go about this?"

"Don't call me Lilykins, March! You know I hate that."

"Pardon me. What would you consider the most favorable mode of operations, *Miss* Lily?"

The others giggled, and Lily grimaced. "See here now, all of you. We got to take this seriously, on account of that overdue bank note. Also, we got to remember this was Daddy's idea, and you know how his ideas usually turn out."

There were sighs and glances up to heaven.

"That's right. Poorly. And it ain't always his fault, either. It wasn't his fault lightning struck the new windmill last August just after he'd finished building it, was it? Nor was it his fault it burned clear to the ground, leaving us without irrigation again. And it wasn't his fault Cricket got palpitations running the treadmill from the creek that he fixed up last month for the same purpose. Daddy just forgot about the heat out here, so our mule's dead, too."

"He must have been nearly ninety, anyway," justified June. "And he ate a lot, lying around the stable all winter."

"But thank goodness Daddy didn't set the horses to the treadmill, or we wouldn't have the means left to do this job." Lily looked at her sisters. "Now, I've noticed there's one thing different about this present scheme, aside from its slight irregularities."

"Yes, Miss Lily?" parroted April.

"The one thing different as I see it," continued Lily, unperturbed, "is that while Daddy thought up this scheme, *we're* in

11

charge of it. Therefore, it might just have the potential for success."

There was a pregnant pause as the Harper girls considered what Lily was intimating. Then May burst into song.

"Lily's right! It could work!" June whooped, jumping into the creek, chemise and all.

The others soon followed suit. It had been a hot day.

"Yippee!"

"San Antonio, here we come!"

  A few days later, plans completed, Lily herded her sisters out of the house. It was a full half hour after Daddy had put away his guitar and he and Mama had retired from the veranda to their bedroom for the night. Daddy usually liked to calm himself down after a hard day with some music. He had a nice voice, too, kind of a sweet, wistful tenor that Mama admired. Sometimes Mama even joined in with her tremulous soprano.

This particular night, the sky was filled with stars, and maybe even the echo of Daddy's guitar, but there was no moon. Lily had checked the almanac for that. Horses saddled, the girls walked them quietly along the creek till they were out of hearing distance of the house. Then they mounted and rode south toward Izzy Henry's spread.

They didn't have to go more than a few miles as the crow flies. The range was open, and most of the ranchers' herds mingled together on the grazing lands. Lily had been out just that afternoon, working as a spotter for the group. She knew where the herds were congregating, and now led her sisters unerringly to the place.

They slowed their mounts to a quiet walk as the dark, drowsing blots materialized before them. There were more cattle than Lily had remembered from the afternoon. Scores of them had sunk to the ground and dotted the undulating landscape like big, black boulders. Others were still on their feet, holding up the night sky.

"How are we going to tell whose is whose in the dark?" whispered April.

"Weren't you paying attention?" Lily snapped. "Tonight we just cut off the first dozen or so, for practice, head them into the cozy, private little canyon back of our place, then sort them out in the morning light."

"You make everything sound so easy, Lily. I'm already sore from sitting astride Dapples here."

"It's your own fault, March. You're out of practice. Why Mama ever suggested you learn to ride sidesaddle last year beats me."

"It's the way ladies do it. And I intend to be a lady!"

"If you don't lower your voice," Lily hissed back, "you'll have lots of time to practice being a lady in jail." She glanced around at the forms of the others in the dark. "Now, you already know how to cut animals out of a herd, all of you. Let's do it!"

There's nothing so dumb as cattle, except maybe sheep, and it took a while to convince this bunch that they were supposed to wake up and move in the middle of the night. Slowly but surely, the idea spread, however, and soon the girls were moving the beasts in the right direction. They made a good half the distance back before Lily thought to check behind her. What she saw made her gasp. They'd picked up a few stragglers: most of the animals that had been spread thinly across the valley had woken and were following the lead of the Harper

13

girls. Instead of the score anticipated, hundreds of Izzy Henry's herd were pursuing them. And the herd was already kicking up a trail of dust, and trampling a telltale path that led inexorably toward the Double H Ranch.

"March!" Lily wailed. "April, May!"

The girls stopped and turned; then fear grew in their eyes.

"What do we do? They're coming closer!" Julie gasped.

"Abandon the lot and run for home," Lily shouted. "Maybe they'll stop!"

The Harper girls spurred their horses and galloped toward the ranch house.

Lily woke in the morning to a deep, rumbling sound, not unlike thunder. But it wasn't the wet season yet. She peeked out the window of the tiny storage room she'd appropriated for a bedroom when she'd gotten fed up on sharing with June and Julie, hoping it was all just a bad dream.

It wasn't. Fences and corrals lay trampled. The entire kitchen garden, everything, was under the feet of cattle. She pulled on her clothes and rushed out to the veranda. The ranch house felt like an island in a sea of black Angus. The sun was barely up, but Daddy was standing there, suspenders sagging around his hips.

"This wasn't exactly what I had in mind when I sprung that last idea, daughter," he managed at last.

"I know, Daddy. I know."

They gave each other a helpless look.

"What you figure Izzy Henry is going to say when he comes searching for his stock?"

"You could blame it on the moon, Daddy."

"Weren't any moon last night, Lily."

Izzy arrived with his ranch hands a few hours later. The whole Harper family, saving Mama, saddled up and helped him move the herd back onto grazing land. It took practically the entire day, and Izzy was still scratching his head in bewilderment when the Harpers and Izzy's hands gathered on a rise to catch their breaths late in the afternoon.

"Never seen anything like this in all my born days. What you figure caused it, Hy?"

Daddy was still wearing the innocent expression he'd been practicing on all day. "Beats me, Izzy. Could be maybe a few Apaches wandered over the border from the territories—" He stopped when he saw his neighbor's terrified face. "But then again, maybe it was just the conjunction of the stars. You know how they sometimes do strange things out here in the middle of nowhere . . ."

Lily turned Checkers away in disgust. This latest setback must have stunted her daddy's imagination. He could usually tell a far better yarn than that. She walked her horse over to where her oldest sisters were talking with Izzy's men.

March was riding sidesaddle again today, in her second-best dress. She and April would pretty themselves for any occasion, and flirt with anything in pants. Lily pulled back on the reins and noticed the admiration of Izzy's top hand, Tom Carter.

Tom had only been around about a year now. He was one of those Eastern boys that had run off to Texas after reading too many dime novels. But he did take naturally to the work, and Lily had seen worse-looking cowpokes. He wasn't overly tall, but lean and muscular, and his thick black hair, brushed back behind his ears and growing long almost to his neck, set off a short, straight nose and a clean-shaven, square jaw.

"Hey, Tom."

" 'Lo, Lily." Then his attention was back on March again, relegating Lily to that very special hell of youngest sisters.

Lily hunted around again for someone else to talk to. April was deep in conversation with Ed Rickerby. That was his given name, but everybody called him Rick on account of he wasn't comfortable with Ed and claimed that Edmund sounded sissified. Rick was considerably older than Tom, maybe five or six whole years, and not near as handsome, with his washed-out brown hair and a busted-looking nose. But he had stylish muttonchop side whiskers, sort of brownish-gingery-colored, and carried the aura of command. He was Izzy's ranch foreman and wore the gray pants with a faded yellow stripe down them from his soldier days. Word was he'd been a hellion for the Confederacy and still couldn't get the losing out of his head.

Lily's other sisters were gnawing on bits of jerky being handed around by Izzy's cook, Ooh-long, a plump, middle-aged Chinaman of great dignity who'd missed his ship in Galveston years ago and was still trying to earn the fare back to his homeland. Lily reached out for a piece, then bit off a satisfying chunk.

"How's the money coming, Ooh-long?"

His smile was resplendent with several gold teeth. "Close, very close, Miss Lily."

Lily didn't scoff—like some of the others—at the idea of his ever being able to save enough money. It upset him, and he was too nice to be upset. But she didn't figure he'd ever get back to China, either. Izzy Henry probably underpaid him on purpose so's he couldn't leave. He was the best cook in this part of the country, and everybody knew it. Also, Mrs. Henry liked the class she thought the cook's proper manners brought to her establishment.

"Ooh-long?"

"Yes, Miss Lily?"

"You ever figure on maybe changing your strategy?"

"What you mean?"

"I mean, you really seem to kind of like it here, elsewise you would've saved up enough to leave long since, instead of getting roaring drunk once a year like everybody knows you do, and losing all your money to gamblers and such—"

His frame stiffened. "If people here knew mah-jongg, I not be losing all the time. I was top mah-jongg man in all Shanghai!"

Lily sighed. "You ain't being realistic, Ooh-long. It takes a different kind of luck to make it out here."

"Your esteemed daddy has not found it yet. How you expect me to?"

"Sometimes I think he's just a born Jonah. But even Jonah got out of the whale's belly after a piece. Maybe Daddy just ain't paid enough dues yet."

"Maybe so, maybe not." The cook gave her another look. "But you smart just the same. I see you smart from when you just the size of rice bowl, ride over to observe Ooh-long cook." He stopped. "What you think I should do next?"

"You ain't getting any younger, Ooh-long. I figure you should give up on China for yourself, but maybe send off for a wife. Bet you anything Izzy would ante up the cash in advance for that."

She could see a spark of interest in the Chinaman's usually flat black eyes. Then Daddy interrupted.

"Socializing's done for the day, daughters. Time to head on home and see to our own mess."

March flounced her head and April was equally put out. Lily could tell that they'd just been getting comfortable with Tom and Rick. Daddy put an end to any protests quickly.

"On account of it was his animals that caused the damage, Izzy's generously offered to send a few of his men over in the morning to help us rebuild the corrals. It being Sunday, and their usual day of rest, I hope you girls plan on thanking them all nicely, and pitching in, too."

The two oldest brightened immediately, and the Harpers went home in reasonable spirits.

It took longer to get the Double H Ranch back into shape than anyone had anticipated. Tom and Rick ended up riding over practically every evening. They'd walk out into the coolness of the setting sun with March and April and a few tools to inspect the fencing. There'd be desultory hammer blows echoing down past the ranch house for a while, then just the silence of the coming night.

Lily took the visits philosophically. Mama puttered anxiously around her cattle-stunted garden until it was too dark to be out anymore. Daddy seemed to ignore the whole issue, as did June and Julie mostly. May was jealous.

On the second Saturday evening after the rustling fiasco, Lily and May sat on the veranda in Daddy and Mama's cane-backed rocking chairs. Lily's feet were up on the railing. She had her whittling knife out, and in between swatting at mosquitoes, she was inspecting an interesting piece of juniper root she'd picked up that afternoon while riding the range.

May had loosed her blond hair around her shoulders. She claimed braids and buns gave her headaches, and always pulled them all out as soon as the evening started to cool down. She was halfheartedly plunking at Daddy's guitar.

"Now we're never going to get to San Antonio, Lily."

"Doesn't bother me. Can't miss what you've never seen."

"Hah! Just wait till you're my age. You'll be singing a different song."

"Can't see how my being sixteen'll change my outlook so much."

"Well, it'll certainly change mine. When you're sixteen, I'll be nineteen, and still stuck here! March and April promised to stand by me, through thick and thin, and here they've gone and snatched the only two reasonable men in the entire county!"

"You're not exactly an old maid yet, May. And even nineteen ain't over the hill. Why, Mama didn't marry Daddy till she was a full twenty!"

But May was still pursuing her own train of thought.

"Didn't you ever want to see where Mama came from? Her daddy was one of the first Anglo traders in San Antonio. He came all the way out from Kentucky with Grandmama. Why, he even fought for an independent Texas!"

"Not at the Alamo. You heard Daddy telling it, how Granddaddy packed up his wife and youngsters and ran like the dickens when Santa Anna's army came trooping up from Mexico. And he didn't come back to pick up the pieces till after it was all over."

"That just proves how smart he was. It wouldn't have done any good if they were all murdered in their beds, would it?"

"What I can't figure," pondered Lily, dismissing her granddaddy's valor, or lack of, completely, "is why they never came to visit us. If they had all that money, and position, and everything? You'd think they'd want to help out their only daughter a little."

May gave Lily a superior glance. "You're still a child, Lily. You keep forgetting that Mama and Daddy eloped. For love!" She sighed at the thought.

Lily sat in the growing dark and swatted more mosquitoes. That had always been a hard one to understand. She loved her daddy right enough, but she couldn't picture him as a heroic figure, one who'd inspire someone like Mama—who must've been really pretty at some point—to leave the comfort of home and family for the questionable pleasures of the Double H Ranch. Especially since Mama never had taken to ranching the way Lily did.

"Did he have more hair then?"

"Who?"

"Daddy, of course."

May grinned through the dark. "They got a wedding tintype taken. Mama has it hidden in her old hope chest. You mean you never snuck a look at it?"

"If it ain't out, I figure it's not my business."

"Daddy was kind of cute, in a serious way."

"But did he have more hair?"

"He had more. And money, too. From being in at the beginning of the California Gold Rush like he was. Kind of at the right spot at the right time for once in his life, since he was stranded out there near Sacramento at the end of the Mexican War." She strummed a celebratory chord on the guitar in honor of the exploit, then worked into a sad Spanish song Daddy always played when he was feeling blue. "The trouble is, I've never been able to understand why he came back at all. And then, why he came back and threw every last piece of gold

19

into buying this place. With more thought, he could've at least gone a little farther north and east, into the *real* hill country, instead of this scruffy borderland. They say there's water everywhere up there, lakes full of it, and the bluebells covering everything so in the spring, you think you'd gone to heaven." Her fingers softly completed the wistful lament.

Lily put away her knife. After serious consideration, she'd decided the root in her hand was perfect as it was, all wavy-grainy like that. Maybe she'd just smooth a smidgen of neat's-foot oil onto its edges. "Daddy's land is good enough for me. Got lots of wide-open spaces to ride out into, and the all-over smell of juniper and sage, and the cactus flowers in the summer—"

A series of giggles coming from down the creek interrupted her train of thought. Lily craned her neck in that direction. "All four of 'em seem to be heading back. I guess they couldn't find anything else to repair tonight."

May opened her mouth to say something, then shut it again.

3

Lily could tell exactly when Daddy started thinking again. It was toward the end of June, about two weeks after things had been cleaned up from the cattle-rustling debacle. There was but six months left to come up with that money the bank wanted—six hundred dollars he'd borrowed for the dam, and then the windmill, then extra stock. If it seemed an impossible sum to her, who'd never seen more than a plugged nickel, she could understand how desperate Daddy must be feeling.

She was sitting on the top rail of the nearest corral, one of Daddy's old wide-brimmed felt hats slung over her head to keep the sun off and the freckles down. Not that the freckles bothered Lily, but they seemed to make quite an impression on her mama. Least, Mama was always trying to get her to rub some of that cucumber compound on them that she and the other girls made every year the pickles decided to grow. March and April used it religiously to improve their complexions to Mama's standards of Anglo San Antonio society. The stuff gave Lily goose bumps.

So she was just sitting there, absently chewing on the tail end of her braid, watching March make a fool of herself, doggedly trying to train Dapples to jump over fence posts like the Eastern ladies did, so she could impress her beau on his next visit. And March didn't even have the benefit of a real Eastern sidesaddle.

On his last couple of evening visits, Tom Carter had been filling up March's head with a bunch of nonsense about the East. He wasn't too bad for a Yankee, but he did talk a lot about where he came from—a place he called the Brandywine Country in some tiny state Lily'd never heard of before. Delaware. Lands, if it was true this Delaware could fit into Texas about three hundred times, it was no wonder he'd left. Lily couldn't imagine being scrunched into a place that small.

Anyway, Tom said that back East, not only did ladies ride sidesaddle but they did it in something called the Hunt, wherein a whole bunch of people got dressed up in red and chased a poor fox all over tarnation, with horns blowing and everything. Lily figured they had to be mighty bored back there. Now, if it was coyotes they were after, that would make a certain amount of sense. But you'd never go hunting coyotes with horns blowing. That noise would scare the critters clean fifty miles away. And then you wouldn't have to bother with the Hunt at all.

It was after March had fallen and dusted her bottom good for the third time that Daddy poked his head out of the stable.

"March! That'll be enough for today. A few more falls and you'll knock what little sense is left in your head clean out of it."

"But, Daddy!"

"Don't talk back, daughter. You put that much energy into something useful, there's no end to what we could accomplish around here. And, Lily, you can stop your snickering and go find the rest of the crew. I don't think March has the strength left for it."

"You got another idea, Daddy? Hope it's better than the last one."

He scowled, and Lily ran.

When all were present and at attention by the usual spot in front of the stable workbench, Daddy surprised them by launching into a lecture on temperance.

"Now, you all know how your mama and I feel about the vicissitudes of drink."

"You referrin' to the Devil's Brew, Daddy?"

"None other, Lily. You know how we don't keep any of that around, and never have."

"Likely couldn't afford it, anyhow. Ooh-long says a really superior brand costs plenty. One that gives you a lift, but don't leave you with a busted head the next few days."

"Lily, I think maybe you're getting too old to be traipsing off visiting Izzy's cook."

"Please, Daddy! Tom and Rick come up here all the time. Besides, I got to see what happens with his mail-order bride! He finally got permission from Mr. Henry and sent off letters last week to San Francisco and Hawaii both, since once he got to liking the idea he decided China was too far."

Daddy sighed. "We'll discuss this later, Lily. What I want to get through your heads here and now is my feelings towards the, uh, subject I been trying to discuss. How I don't necessarily condone its use. Save for medicinal purposes, of course. Just so's you all understand our next little project."

"Has it something to do with the wagon full of cracked corn you brought back from the mill in Fredericksburg yesterday, Daddy?" asked May. "And the sacks of sugar?"

"And those odds and ends of copper you've been collecting?" April inquired.

"I thought the corn was to fatten Mama's chickens and ducks," Julie said, accusation in her tone.

"And where'd you get the money for the corn, Daddy, if you don't have anything to give the bank in San Antonio, and nothing for new dress cloth?"

"I am still in charge of the finances in this family, Miss March. And the bank in Fredericksburg don't necessarily need to know about the bank in San Antone, does it?"

"You took out another loan!" June exclaimed.

He looked at his daughters with chagrin. "Thank the Lord none of you is a bank officer, that's all I can say. Never let a man get a word in edgewise. There's a reason for all of this. A good one."

He waited until he had their undivided attention again.

"Now then, as Ooh-long noticed, there's good whiskey and bad whiskey, and the good stuff's hard to come by outside of San Antone. Even when you can get it, the price ain't always right." He paused. "Seems to me this might be a situation we could rectify."

"You gonna make some moonshine, Daddy?"

" 'Tain't illegal, Lily, noways. 'Tain't hardly even immoral, depending on your point of view. You don't need to refer to it by that derogatory name. And you all don't need to go getting your backs up about it, like last time. Then on the other hand, what with the North's excise taxes on homemade brew . . ."

He caught their puzzled expressions. "That there's some extra money the Yankee government can charge you per bottle—if they find out you're selling it. Money them carpetbaggers'll send straight back to President Grant, if they don't line their own pockets with it first." He considered again. "On the other hand, it ain't something we need to be telling the neighbors about, either. Just in case." Daddy stopped. "It's only commonsense capitalism, finding a market and going after it. I'm going to make some fine whiskey."

"Who you going to sell it to?" Lily really wanted to know. "Mr. Henry's cowpokes? Don't seem like it would be worth the effort."

"I am not going to sell it to Izzy's cowpokes, Lily, neither am I planning on selling it to your precious Ooh-long."

"Then who are you going to sell it to, Daddy?" It was March, figuring the odds, as usual. "The only other population out here is the occasional Indian. But everybody knows it makes them crazy. Are you planning on starting an uprising, Daddy?"

"Let me talk!"

They did.

"Ain't none of you figured yet who else lives out here?" He stared at their blank faces. "Well, I'll tell you. Yankee soldiers, that's who. Up at the forts."

"Oh." It was a general sigh.

"It couldn't possibly be considered wrong helping to dissipate the Yankees, could it?" April was no doubt thinking about former Confederate lieutenant Ed Rickerby.

"That was my feelings on the subject, daughter, in a nutshell. Almost like a patriotic act, it might be." He was actually smiling. "Just let me show you these plans I've been working on. I know they're good, because I did some research on the subject back in my California days. Once we get the still built, up in Dead Man's Canyon, it won't take but a week or so to get us some fine product ready for business. Then it's only a matter of bottling it and lugging it up to Fort Mason, maybe even as far as Fort McKavett."

They bent over his sketch to see how easy it would really be.

Between the usual rounds of riding out to check the fences and move the remaining cattle around to fresh grazing and water, it took somewhat longer than estimated to get Daddy's still built.

The main hopper had to be constructed out of canyon rock and daub. This hopper was to set a big copper tub into—one of Mama's washtubs—with a small oven-like fireplace underneath. Next was figuring out how to connect the finished hopper by copper tubes to a series of barrels the vapor would flow and condense through as it was distilled.

When it was done, complete with its peculiar, inverted funnel over the main hopper, and a copper condensing "snake" spiraling through the air, Lily figured it to be the strangest idea her daddy had yet cooked up. But Daddy, he was all smiles and enthusiasm as he adjusted the little rivulets of water that he guided through wooden troughs from the trickling branch of Hollering Woman Creek that ran partway through the canyon. The water was supposed to flow around the copper to cool things down and turn the corn vapor into alcohol. At least, that's how Daddy explained it. He figured sure and certain this project could never go wrong. The very afternoon they hauled out the supplies to inaugurate the still, he'd already begun adding up the money he intended to make from it.

"We're gonna start us out with a first batch of about fifty gallons, daughters. We siphon that off into these quart bottles

I bought, that'll give us two hundred quarts to cart off up to the Yankees. We plug in a cork, slap on these labels I had printed up, and we'll be in the money in no time."

Lily was examining the box of labels they'd just unloaded into the canyon. "Nice-looking labels you got here, Daddy. 'Pride of the West.' Catchy name, too. How much it cost you to have them printed up? With that nice picture of the Longhorn's head and all?"

Daddy was obviously pleased with her admiration. "It wasn't hardly anything, Lily. Rex Barker, the printer down to Fredericksburg, he done them up for practically nothing, plus the promise of a few steady jugs for his private use. He claims the saloons have been getting pricey."

"How many thousand you got here, Daddy?"

"Just ten. I figured that would give us a decent start."

"You planning on us cooking up ten thousand quarts of moonshine?"

"Please, Lily, prime whiskey. Pride of the West."

"What are you selling it for, Daddy?"

Daddy looked at June, who'd been standing nearby. "Fifty cents the quart."

June did some rapid calculations in her head. Her facility with arithmetic often surprised the others, as it never did seem to match up with her flightiness. "That means we stand to make a hundred dollars a week. If we can sell it all."

"Oh, it will sell, all right."

"That also means," March added, "in six weeks or so, nothing going wrong"—she squinted at the still through the hot sun—"nothing going wrong, we could clear up your bank note in six weeks."

"Less expenses," Daddy added quickly.

"Just how much in expenses?" March asked suspiciously.

"Never you mind. By fall and the rains, we'll be sitting pretty, that's all." And Daddy went to toss the first sack of sugar into the hopper.

· · ·

It turned out the still had to be watched over like a baby, night and day, once the mash had taken to fermenting. It wasn't to help the whiskey so much as to keep the fire going steady, and to keep sparks from spreading out and setting the dry grass around the canyon alight. That wouldn't be a help to anyone, especially since the ranch house was downwind of it. Turns were taken, and it was Lily's again four days later, when the stuff was starting to brew up something ferocious.

Lily walked Checkers into the canyon, then hobbled him to graze the best he could while she relieved April. Her sister had seen her coming and was already seated on her own horse, anxious to leave. She held a handkerchief up to her nose delicately.

"I declare, Lily, I do hope Daddy makes his money on this fast. I never smelled anything worse in my life!"

"Did you check the brew?"

"Mercy! I wouldn't go near that contraption, save to shove in more wood!"

Lily grinned, waved goodbye, and sauntered over to the still. She eased the funnel off the top and watched as the mash sat there, bubbling and glowering in the afternoon heat. Lily wrinkled her nose. It was a mite strong. She picked up a stick and poked at the mess tentatively, almost expecting something to jump out at her. Nothing did, but she met more resistance than she expected. She poked some more, then managed to pull out a long, skinny object. She looked closer. A rattler, cooked to perfection. The poor critter must have inched up the side, then fallen in, drunk on the fumes. Lily debated removing it, then decided it might just add some character to the brew and let it sink back in. There was no way she'd ever sample any of these results.

Lily checked the fire, then settled onto her back near the still, her hat covering her face. Maybe this time, Daddy's plan would really work out.

• • •

The whiskey had a nice, pale-brown tone when they bottled it a few days later. Daddy could hardly wait for the job to be done. He'd gotten them out to the canyon by sunup so he could head north to Fort Mason as soon as possible. It was a good forty miles, and he wouldn't be back till late the next day, no matter how you looked at it. He paced around nervously now, supervising labels being glued, corks being shot into full bottles. It probably never occurred to him that he might speed up the process by helping out himself.

"Calm yourself, Daddy, we've only got a few gallons left to deal with."

He scowled up at the sun rising in the sky and paced some more.

Lily glued her last Pride of the West label. She took pains to put it on squarely, nicely centered. It was good to take an interest in your work. "Sure you don't want any company on this trip, Daddy? It might be nice to have someone to talk to—"

"No, no. You've all got your chores laid out for you. And the fresh batch of mash to tend. Besides, I don't want my daughters connected by sight to this enterprise."

"That's mighty sweet of you, Daddy, protecting our reputations like that."

Daddy glanced at March, unsure whether he'd actually detected sarcasm in her voice. He shook it off, then paced some more, finally stopping to nestle the bottles into the protective hay covering the wagon bed.

"Right, then. I'm away. See you watch over your mother for me. And for heaven's sake, don't let on what I'm doing!"

The girls gave their daddy scandalized looks, then lined up to stretch their necks and give him goodbye kisses. He bent down from the buckboard seat to acknowledge their homage, then cracked his whip.

"Don't stop for any wandering Indians!"

"Have a safe trip!"

After he'd started off, the Harper girls shared a sigh of relief. "Is it breakfast time yet? We'd better get home to hold Mama's hand."

Daddy got back after sundown the next night. Lily jumped off the veranda, where she'd been oiling some harness, to catch the horses.

"How did it work? Did the Yankees like it? Are we gonna get your debts paid off?"

She couldn't see his face in the dark, but heard his groans as he jumped to the ground and stretched.

"Well?"

"Well, there's been a little hitch in our plans, but nothing too serious."

By now the other girls were running out in their night-dresses. They surrounded Daddy, but he shook his head.

"Tomorrow. I've got to let your mama know I'm back."

Daddy showed them their profits the next day. They consisted of a fistful of useless scrip, five brass buttons, and a series of I.O.U.'s.

"But, Daddy, I don't understand." It usually took Julie a while to figure things out. "Where's the money?"

"The soldiers ain't been paid in months. But they liked the product all right, and swore to stand by their debts like gentlemen."

April was dumbfounded. "And you believed them? You took a bunch of Yankees' word, and just gave away all those quarts—"

"Now, April, not all Yankees are lying skunks—"

"Hush up, March. We already know Tom Carter comes from money and he's been educated, and he doesn't count!"

"Girls, girls. There's a certain setup time in any enterprise. You have to get your customers' trust, and—"

A thought suddenly clicked in Lily's head. "Just a minute, Daddy," she broke in. "I just want to get something straight. How did you come by that gold out in California?"

"What's that got to do with anything?"

"I just need to know, is all."

Daddy looked pained.

"Did you dig it up?"

"Lily."

They were all staring at him now. His shoulders sagged farther. "All right, then. It was a poker game. The best hand I ever had in my life. With my luck, everyone thought I had to be bluffing, and the stakes just kept going up. Finally I won Black Bill Mooney's entire mine. I sold it back to him later at a reasonable price, naturally, like any honest man would, but it still gave me my stake, and I hightailed it home." He straightened up before the eyes boring through him. "And I ain't never played poker since!"

"That depends, Daddy."

"What are you alluding to, Lily?"

"It just seems to me that maybe poker's more of a way of life than a game, Daddy."

The second batch of liquor was tended with a lot less enthusiasm than the first. Maybe that's why when the still blew up about midnight on the third day after the mash set in, nobody was as upset as they might have been.

Lily had been up when it happened, prowling around the sleeping house hunting for something to eat and worrying. She'd just dug into a bowl of cold stew on the veranda when she saw the flash in the sky from the canyon. It was impressive, even if you couldn't hear much more than a mild boom way down here. But Daddy was up there tending the still. Lily dropped the bowl, jumped into a pair of britches, grabbed a lantern, and ran out for Checkers.

Miraculously, there'd been no fire. Just the one boom and flare of light, then the whole still had caved in on itself. Daddy

30

was lying nearby, and Lily ran to prop him up. "You all right, Daddy?"

He nodded like it hurt, and she saw one single tear trickle down his scruffy cheek. Poor man.

"You weren't going to see any money out of those Yankees anyway, Daddy."

"But it was so promising!"

Lily pulled him up and brushed off his clothing solicitously. "Just let me get this lantern lit and maybe we can figure out what happened."

What had happened was that a monstrously fat prairie dog had gotten lost and stuck in the main pipe, causing the distilled vapors to build up pressure. Lily pulled the prairie dog out by its squat, singed tail and stared at it.

"They always were curious critters, prairie dogs. Just like people. I hope this one didn't have a family."

"Is that all you got to say, Lily?"

"All that's necessary. Come on home to bed, Daddy. Mama doesn't sleep well nights without you."

The Harper girls were gathered by the tool bench again. This time, Daddy had a new display for them. It wasn't but ten days past the last fiasco. He'd been busy. It being the first of August and only five months left till foreclosure, he had to be. Daddy was damp all over from the ungodly heat, but he ignored the sweat beading him from his bald head down as he waited for the buzz of curiosity to simmer into silence.

"I figure it's time you girls learned to be a trifle more adept with firearms. So I gathered together all the shootin' implements we got here at the ranch. I also set up a little practice range back in Dead Man's Canyon."

"What are we meant to aim at, the remnants of the still?"

"March." It was a quiet admonishment, but it didn't hush the rest.

"It would have been the perfect place to hide Izzy Henry's stock," said April. "Why, we couldn't even hear the still when it blew!"

"There'll be no more talk of either the still or Izzy Henry's stock. Particularly the stock. That was a lapse of judgment on my part. Looking back, I figure we're all of us round about here in pretty much the same boat. And I don't intend to ever be accused of preying on my closest neighbors and friends."

"It wasn't preying then, Daddy," piped up June. "Two months ago it was just a little 'loan' to tide us over."

"Turning fifteen recently appears to have limbered up your mouth some, June. I seem to remember preferring you more silent, like your mama."

Lily spoke before she thought. "Mama lost her spunk years back, Daddy. I think the busted dam was the last straw."

"Was it my fault she was using the privy at that moment, Lily? Was it?"

"Sorry, Daddy."

"She's been constipated ever since."

"June!"

Daddy's face had turned beet-red. He stretched his wiry body, possibly in an attempt to gather the reins of control back into his own hands again. It was getting harder every month.

"As I was saying. Our financial situation hasn't improved one iota since our last thwarted attempts. The summer's getting hotter, the land drier. The sorry stock we got left won't be

32

worth slaughtering for our own larder come autumn if things don't change. And if we eat our own stock, pitiful though it be, that leaves us with no means whatsoever."

"Why don't we move, Daddy?" asked May. "Someplace nice, like San Antonio. I'll bet Granddaddy Winslow would forgive all and give you a job in his establishment. I'll bet he's even got a genuine piano like you always said you'd buy for me."

"I don't even know if the old goat is still alive, and anyways I wouldn't go crawling back to him, ever. Neither would I leave my land. So you can just forget about your piano for a while, May. And that's final!"

The girls shuffled a little, the swishing of their skirts adding the slightest breeze to cut through the stifling midday steam. Lily figured May was just trying to improve the male ratio a little. And that piano business, well, May had been begging after one for years, ever since the time they'd been to Izzy Henry's spread for a barbecue and she'd seen his wife's. May could probably even learn to play it. She was already almost better than Daddy on the guitar.

"What then, Daddy?" Lily asked. "How you figure our shooting ability's going to change things any?"

"If you'd all just give a man a chance to talk!" He was roaring now. Lily shut up. "Now, I've been studying the local terrain and drawing some maps of our land, and Izzy's, too." He pulled a crinkled specimen off his workbench and waved it under their noses. "Whilst the once and future railroad seems likely to miss us entire, there's still hope." He pointed to a dark black line he'd scrawled over to the east of their property. "Any one of you know what this represents?"

He met blank faces.

Daddy smiled. "It happens to represent the direct route of the Stage Express between Abilene and San Antone. I got to know a piece of this selfsame trail on my trip up to Fort Mason. And I happen to figure that the stage comes within eight or ten miles of our ranch house each and every week. I also happen to know the stage is what carries the Yankee soldiers' payroll, which is imminently due." There was a hushed silence.

"Can any of you stretch your minds to cover those facts? Can any of you come up with a reasonable conclusion?"

Julie leaned back against a splintery joist and began to cry.

"What in blue blazes are you snuffling about, girl?"

"I know what she's upset about, Daddy, and for once I agree!" March stood tall, with her shoulders pulled back and her bosom thrust forward in her old blue gingham dress. Then she exploded. "I won't do it! We won't any of us do it! Rustling was one thing, and it didn't get us to San Antonio, but it did get me Tom Carter. The moonshine was smelly and nasty, too, and even put you further into debt, though it didn't hurt us beyond that. But, but—all my trouble to learn to be a lady, and now this. Ladies don't rob stagecoaches!"

Julie was sobbing in earnest now, whispering to herself, "Wrong, wrong."

"Ain't you figured out yet we're two months closer to losing every bit of home and security you been brought up with, daughter? Whose veranda you plan to do your stitching on when ours is gone?" Julie stopped in mid-sob, her eyes wide. Daddy turned to the others. "Whose garden is your mama going to grow her vegetables in? And you, Lily. Whose horse you plan on riding when the bank sends a repossessor in to haul off your Checkers?"

"Why, they wouldn't never—"

"They would. And they will. In five months. That brings us to winter, if you hadn't worked that out, either. You think we can maybe just camp out in the hills with no roof over our heads when the snows start coming? What would that do to your mama's delicate health?"

That got their full attention. "Now, I'm open to any reasonable alternatives any of you can come up with, but if you ain't got any, we'll have to make do with this."

Daddy leaned back against the workbench, worn out. Lily

could tell he hadn't ever meant to lay all of those worries on their heads, but they'd forced him to it. Nobody was going to take away the ranch or Checkers. Right or wrong, she was in on this one. Her mind sped on to the ramifications of the job. There was only one thing about the new project that troubled her, once she'd worked past the larcenous part. "I won't be shooting any people, Daddy. That's for sure and certain."

Daddy had regained some of his aplomb. "Lily! How could you even suggest such a thing! It's just a general familiarity with the weapons I'm requesting. So you don't look like green-horns. Just the subtle appearance of a threat."

March was beginning to recover, too. She took a deep breath and pulled out a threadbare, lace-trimmed handkerchief, one of Mama's from the old days, embroidered with her maiden initials. Thrusting the square of linen at Julie, who still had need of it, March shared a private look with April. Then she cleared her throat ever so delicately.

"They carry ready spending money on the stage, don't they, Daddy? Especially for the Yankees' pay?"

"It was my general understanding, yes. Gold coin."

"Ready cash money, *gold*, is easier to hide and spend than Izzy Henry's cattle. And less trouble, too," March continued.

"The thought had crossed my mind."

April picked up from her sister. "And those Yankees owe you at least a hundred dollars, which we'll never see, since you've got no cause to trek back up there with the still gone and all."

"They sure as certain do, the prevaricating scoundrels! And may their heads still be aching from the results!"

"Not that they'd pay you anyway, without fresh goods in hand," June added.

March ignored both June's comment and Daddy's vehemence. "And we'd be doing this on our own, without your immediate assistance, because if they don't hang female rustlers, they wouldn't hang female robbers, either."

Daddy was beginning to beam. "I knew I'd passed on some intelligence to my daughters. I'd be available for background planning, of course, for strategy—"

"That's all right, Daddy," said March, already marshaling her sisters from the stable. "Maybe it's better if you just leave the details to us."

🖝 This time, Lily was in charge of the costumes. There were all of Daddy's old britches and shirts like they'd used the last time, but that had been at night and no one'd been too particular about their attire. Now they'd be in the clothes longer and in broad daylight. March and April—for that matter, all the rest of the older girls—wanted their debut before their public to be convincing, and sartorially correct. It was kind of hard with the material Lily had to work with.

True, nothing had ever been thrown away out here. There was a selection of their father's under- and outerwear going back to before his marriage. Lily wouldn't even have been surprised had she come upon a teeny union suit from his baby days. She couldn't imagine Daddy ever without his union suit, even in the heat of summer. They came in whites and grays, of course, but given the option, he'd always gone for red. This small fact pleased Lily, almost gave her daddy an image of strength and solidity in her mind. There was something he'd followed through on, successfully.

The twenty years' worth of discards surrounding her in the bunkhouse were a sorry lot, however. Lily doggedly went on with her task, making six piles of each item. They'd need handkerchiefs, too, big ones to mask their faces. There'd been talk of going for fake beards and mustaches as well, but Lily didn't think the horses would take to having their manes and tails trimmed. Instead, she'd collected a fire-blackened hunk of charcoal. She stopped her sorting for a minute to pull it out of her shirt pocket and dab it at her upper lip experimentally.

Lily scrutinized the effect in a tiny piece of broken mirror. She started giggling, but stopped when she saw her mother's puzzled face reflected behind her own.

"What in the world are you doing, Lily?"

The blackening was hastily smudged off onto her shirtsleeve. "Playing, Mama."

"Oh, dear. I knew we should have tried for just one more baby, to keep you company. But your daddy said enough was enough."

"He was probably right, Mama. What are you doing out here, anyway? I thought Julie was in charge of the chickens this week."

"Well, you know Julie. She just isn't conscientious enough, except with those samplers of hers. All her good intentions seem to disappear right into them. I usually go through the hay a second time for the eggs she missed. I was thinking of making a cake."

"But we're between birthdays for a while."

"I just felt like a cake, Lily. Your daddy's been acting a mite downhearted lately, and I thought it might cheer him up at supper."

"You still think a plumb lot of Daddy, don't you, Mama. Even after everything."

"Why, whatever do you mean by 'everything,' Lily?"

"Well, he ain't exactly made a success of his spread like Izzy Henry did, Mama. Take Mrs. Izzy, for instance. She dresses up in fine clothes every day of the year, and gets to San Antonio once a season, and—"

"Lily, I do wish you wouldn't use 'ain't' so often. It isn't becoming to a young lady. And I don't know what gets into you to just ride over to the Henrys', uninvited, whenever it suits you—"

"I like to talk to Ooh-long. He's been teaching me to cook Chinese, although he does say it doesn't taste like anything in Shanghai, on account of he hasn't the right accoutrements. Things like soy sauce. And hoisin sauce. He craves mightily for them. Just turns up his nose at a good mess of barbecue."

Mama gave her an odd look. "I really don't know where you came from sometimes, Lily. You're not at all like your sisters." She cast a glance at the piles of clothes spread around her daughter. "And here I thought you were long past dress-up and playacting. And you just entirely missed dolls, like they never meant anything to you. You'd always rather haul a pet iguana to bed with you."

"They never did, and I'd still rather. You notice how the iguanas are getting scarce around these parts, though, Mama? You think maybe we put too many of 'em into stew when the garden burnt out last summer?"

Her mother shuddered at the remembrance. Then Lily had another thought. It wasn't often she'd get her mama to herself like this, for a talk.

"Don't you miss San Antonio, Mama?"

Mama began her egg search. "Once you make your bed, you've got to lie in it, Lily Harper. That's something you'll understand better when you get a little older. And your daddy has tried harder than any man around here. You must always honor him for that fact, and because he is your father." Mama straightened up from an empty nest and left the bunkhouse, eggless.

Lily leaned back against a bale of hay. Even this far along in their latest endeavor, she couldn't always wipe out all the second thoughts that tended to come over her. Mama had taught them all the Ten Commandments when they were small. "Honor thy father and thy mother" was right up there near the top of the list. Before "Thou shalt not steal" and the business about not coveting thy neighbor's property. But none of the Commandments had come home to roost before the last month or so. And now the father that they were supposed to honor and obey was outright advocating that they forget about some of the rest of the list. Did things work that way?

Lily shrugged to herself. She hadn't ever coveted any of Izzy's cattle, and neither was she anxious for somebody else's gold. She didn't need any new dresses or a husband. But she did not want Daddy to lose his ranch. It was burnt-out and sorry, but it was all he had. And he had tried doing everything the right way, for years. Also, no bank repossessor was going near her horse. Besides, March said all the money on those stages was "insured" by the Wells Fargo company, even the Yankee Army's. She said that meant the true owners never really lost anything in a robbery.

It had to be done. If she saw a deadly scorpion crawling on one of her sisters, there wouldn't be much point in yelling and screaming about what might happen. She'd just have to walk over, flick the varmint off, and grind it into the dust, like she'd done more than once. This bank note was growing into one monstrous scorpion in Lily's mind. It had to be gotten rid of. And if the doing could also be interesting, well, that was all right, too.

Satisfied for the moment, Lily bent over her work again.

☞ The target practice was going along apace. Every afternoon, just before supper, all six girls trundled off into Dead Man's Canyon to work at the range Daddy had set up, centered, after all, on the ruins of the still. It was a good site, because even though the gunshots thundered around and around the surrounding cliffs of the box canyon in increasing echoes, for some reason the noise never got beyond to the ranch house, and Mama.

The three oldest were serious about their efforts. It was June and Julie who were the worst. They didn't seem to have the aptitude for the job. June went at it dramatically enough, maybe too dramatically. She'd make wide sweeps with the gun at everything but the target, till the rest of them were ducking for fear of their lives. Come the day, they'd have to be sure her weapon remained unloaded.

And Julie. Given her druthers, she'd rather be on the ranch-house veranda stitching up one of her silly samplers. She'd already produced dozens of them, and their mottoes cluttered up the ranch-house walls. Things like **HOME SWEET HOME** or **HOPE SPRINGS ETERNAL IN THE HUMAN BREAST** or **AN HONEST MAN'S THE NOBLEST WORK OF GOD.** Her current offering was to be **NO LEGACY IS SO RICH AS HONESTY.** She'd gotten as far as "No legacy," with just the other words penciled in, when the current business had begun. Now Lily wondered if Julie would have the heart to finish this particular stitching, considering as how stagecoach robbing didn't actually come under the heading of honesty.

At any rate, Julie's heart surely wasn't in the project. Or maybe it was her conscience still acting up. Take how she held Daddy's old Sharps single-barrel rifle. He'd had it so long, the brass of the fancy Spanish engraving around the breech was almost worn smooth from polishing and use. But Julie didn't understand the affection that had gone into that, had no feelings for the rifle at all, like Lily did. And she sure as shooting didn't know how to even snuggle it up to her shoulder.

"Lower the stock a couple of inches, Julie," Lily coached. "Pull that trigger now and you'll lose a few teeth!"

The last comment came too late. Julie pulled the trigger anyway, the barrel jumping in a wide arc. Lily ran up and removed the implement of destruction from her sister's grasp. It was easy. Julie'd automatically loosened her death grip and sat down backwards in the dust when it went off.

"Honestly, Julie. You'll never get the hang of it that way!"

"Let me be, Lily! I'm fed up on coercion!" She was rubbing her chin, tears in her eyes once more, before struggling up to slap at the dust on the bottom of her worn dress.

Lily turned to March. "Forget the rifle for Julie. We'll let her carry that cute pearl-handled pistol Daddy bought for Mama a few Christmases back."

March was doubtful. "It might work. If we keep her behind us."

"We'd better plan on that for sure."

June flung down her Winchester. "I've had enough of this for today. Isn't it suppertime yet?"

Lily guessed the scenario didn't suit June's craving for play-acting anymore. She pushed up the brim of her hat and glanced at the sky. "Probably. If you're in a hurry for more beans."

Mama had made her cake after all, but it came out kind of hard and flat without the usual six or eight egg whites she liked to whip up into the batter. Daddy didn't seem to mind.

41

He just beamed at her on its presentation, wiped the sweat from his brow, then covered his slab with molasses and treated it like pancakes.

Tom and Rick, as hot and damp as everyone else, arrived before the Harpers had finished, so they sat down to slices of the disaster, too. Rick slung a forkful in his mouth with apparent relish and swallowed. He nudged a few crumbs from his whiskers.

"I'm heading over to Fredericksburg tomorrow, Mr. Harper. Anything I can get for you?"

Daddy considered. "A recent copy of the *San Antonio Express* might be nice. Ain't seen a copy of a paper so long, begin to feel almost isolated out here."

Lily gave her daddy a sharp glance. What was he up to? He'd just been to Fredericksburg last month over the moonshine business and hadn't bothered to bring a paper back then. Besides, he hadn't shown any interest in outside events since General Ulysses S. Grant had been elected President. And when that news had come through last fall, Daddy'd just shrugged and said as how in spite of Grant the sun still shone and the water still flowed in Texas, though Grant might see to this insubordination after his inauguration. Well, the sun still shone all right, but maybe Grant had seen about the water. Hollering Woman Creek was getting drier every blessed day.

"Hear any news from the local U.S. Cavalry?" Daddy was asking Rick.

"I heard the poor sods out at Fort Mason and Fort McKavett are sweltering away in this heat. Those woolen blues sure are a natural disadvantage out there." He grinned at the idea of his old enemies' discomfort. "But their government pay's due in soon, then they'll be hell-for-leather down to Mason and Fredericksburg trying to spend it all in a weekend."

Lily finally caught the logic behind the desultory conversation. The coach's schedule might be noted in the newspaper. She glanced across the table to March and caught her sister's blue eyes lighting up. Rick's words hadn't fallen on deaf ears.

42

Tom crammed the last piece of dry cake into his mouth, nearly choked, then pushed back his chair and rose with a gallant nod of thanks to Mama. He must have seen the spark in March's eyes as well, but interpreted it differently.

"I noticed on the way in, there's another piece of fencing down by the southwest of your place. It could be that some of those maverick Longhorns the Apache have been driving in this direction were playing with it. Anyone care to walk on out and inspect the damage with me?"

Three other chairs scraped back simultaneously; then March, April, and their young men disappeared.

Lily, toying with her cake, stayed put. "Daddy?"

"Yes, daughter?"

"You know how we were discussing what you called alternatives? Why don't we consider capturing some of those Longhorns, if they're really hereabouts? They're free for the taking, and we could drive them up to Kansas this fall just as easy as nothing."

Daddy gave her a scowl. "First, there's Tom's words to consider, and his motivation. Personally, I don't think there're any Longhorns about. They're mostly all down in the Big Thicket, and have been for years. Secondly, there ain't no Apache about herding any. That's just the way news builds around here. Everybody's been talking Injuns since I made the suggestion to Izzy during our roundup of his stock. Even over in Fredericksburg the folks have been giving the local half-breeds suspicious looks. Finally, there's nothing as tough as a wild Longhorn."

"Easterners don't seem to care how tough their beef is, Daddy, long as it's beef."

"I been trying for years, Lily, to stock up quality merchandise. Tender beef on the hoof. You want me to throw all that effort out?"

"Well, if the Longhorns are out there, and they're truly free, and there's a market for them—even hides—it seems to me it would be easier and honester than—"

May stood up suddenly. "Help me clear the table, Lily. It's our turn tonight."

Lily saw her daddy's face turn red. She guessed from that her idea wasn't a working alternative. Her mama noticed nothing. She just smiled at him sweetly.

"There's no need for you to hurry, Hy dear. Have the last piece of dessert."

When the supper chores were finished, Lily headed out to the veranda, took her usual spot in Daddy's rocking chair, and propped her feet up on the railing. June wandered out and sniffed.

"I declare, Lily, your feet up like that, you look exactly like one of them boys Daddy's always wished he'd sired."

Lily didn't budge her feet an inch, just leisurely watched June prepare her skirts prior to sitting down in the chair next to her. June's petticoats rustled, and the faded pink cotton clung to them a moment. Settled at last, she began to wave a palmetto fan in her hand.

"I don't care what you say, Miss June Bug. It's a sight easier and more comfortable than those skirts you like to flounce around in. And that fan don't do much more than shove the hot air over to me."

June waved the fan harder. "Honestly, Lily, the way you almost spit out our latest business endeavor in front of Mama tonight—"

"I was just trying a last-ditch stand, like we all ought to be thinking about. Anyway, Mama didn't catch on to a thing. She never does."

"Still and all . . ." June rocked forward to peer up at the sky. "Another clear night. There must be a million stars out there. And one of them's meant for me. I just know it. I can feel it in my bones."

It was Lily's turn to sniff. June had never seen any playacting in her entire life, yet from little on up, she'd wanted to be an actress. Mama had told her stories about the troupes that used

44

to come through San Antonio in her girlhood. June had memorized the bits of plots her mother remembered from works such as *The Indian Princess, Rip Van Winkle*, or *Fashion*. Neither money nor a beau would've gotten her cooperation in Daddy's current scheme, but the promise of seeing a real, genuine performance in San Antonio did the trick, all right.

"I've been thinking, Lily," June said. "Perhaps what's wanted in our little charade is a bit more drama. Something to make it more effective."

"You mean besides the guns?"

"Indians. You notice how the subject of Indians suddenly keeps reappearing? And the Comanche and Apache haven't been anywhere near Gillespie County in years, not in any number."

Lily waited for her sister to get to the point.

"Well, what if we dressed as Indians instead of bandits? Or at least one or two of us. We could swoop down in war paint, shouting and hollering, and scare that coach clear across the county line."

"I thought we wanted to stop it, not just scare it away."

"Oh, pooh. You haven't an exciting bone in your body. You just go about everything so carefully. Like an old stick-in-the-mud."

"At least I get my piece of the business done with. I've got the costumes ready enough. And I don't need any more target practice. How are you and Julie getting on with the surveillance part? Been up by the stagecoach road yet?"

The fan was working double time again. "You know it's practically impossible to ride out almost ten miles and back in the middle of the blazing sun this time of the season."

"This time of the season's when the payload for the U.S. Army posts is coming through. We ought to at least have a good ambush spot picked out. And a place to hide before the stage driver and passengers get their wits back about them."

"You worry too much."

Lily kicked her feet off the railing and got up. "It's not worry.

45

It's just that somebody's got to put some thought into the project. March and April can't see past their young men. The rest of you—I just don't know, sister. The Lord better be watching down on us when we try to pull this off, that's all I can say."

"Why, that's almost blasphemous, Lily."

"I don't see why. The way I've started to figure it, the Yankees deserve a little payback."

"But those soldiers are protecting us from marauding Indians!"

"They're still Yankees. And they still haven't got their due. I.O.U.'s, hah!"

June perked up. "Of course! We could be Masked Avengers, not just common stagecoach robbers! That casts a whole different light on the drama."

"So it does. It might even get you to do your share of the work."

And Lily rolled up her pants and went down to the creek to cool her toes in what was left of the water.

The fresh approach to the robbery went over well with the rest of the Harper girls the next day. June had been sleeping on it and, with March and April's assistance, came up with a few slogans to paint on signs to be displayed provocatively the day of the deed. They argued for a while over phrasing, but

Julie came to the rescue with several pithy mottoes: "Tyranny is the worst of treasons"; "Rebellion to tyrants is obedience to God." Together, they added "Down with U. S. Grant!" and "Yankees, Go Home!"

Julie and June were still procrastinating over their surveillance mission, so Lily offered to go with them. After the noon meal, the three set off to the east, the two older girls with demure bonnets on their heads to keep off the hot sun, Lily with her usual old brown slouch hat of Daddy's.

It was a long ride, and the horses weren't the only ones gasping by the time the girls arrived at the edge of the dusty trail that passed for a road in those parts. True, there wasn't any cactus or sagebrush growing in the middle of it, but aside from that, only the ruts from occasional wagons and coaches defined it.

Lily examined the level stretch that bounded their family land.

"Too flat. We'll have to head north a piece." She squinted through the sun. "Maybe that hill half a mile up."

Julie and June fanned themselves with their handkerchiefs, then gave up on that and just wiped down their faces and necks.

"I never knew stagecoach robbing was such hard work," complained June. "I thought we could just get dressed up, ride out here one day, and do it. This is as bad as riding after cattle with Daddy."

"A woman's work is never done," sighed the other.

"Where *do* you get all your sayings, Julie?" Lily was genuinely curious.

Julie straightened on her mount. "If you took the time to read some of Mama's books, maybe you'd elevate your mind, too."

Lily didn't bother to answer. She just prodded her horse and headed up the trail. It rose to meet the hill she'd spied, then, as she'd hoped, almost precipitously slid down the other side.

And there sat a low but welcoming butte. She rode up into its shade, then slowly made its circumference.

To the rear was an overhang where they and their horses could wait out of sight, in comfort. Above the overhang was another crevice, deeper and darker, going into the butte. A cave? Lily edged Checkers back from the overhang, stood up in her stirrups, and just managed to peek into the darkness. There was a cave! Although its entry point was small, it seemed to widen out behind. And off to the west a creek ran straight from the low, green-spotted hills. It would be the natural exit point, their horses running through water and leaving no footprints till they reached the safety of the hills. Still, if their prey decided to pursue, they'd be in full view for some distance. Lily pulled at the tail end of her braid and began worrying it. She turned at her sisters' approach.

"I surely hope this will do," Julie said.

"It's good, but not perfect. There's something troubling me about it."

"Well, let's water the horses over there and let you worry while we head home. I've had enough," grumbled June.

"We don't do it right, we'll get caught," Lily said. "Wouldn't help anybody then."

That misty look was already filming over Julie's eyes. "And poor Mama would die of shame."

"And poor Daddy would lose everything," added Lily. "Let's go."

Lily came up with the solution in the middle of the night. It was too hot to sleep, anyway, and somehow a trail of red ants had found their way into her room to torture her. She sat up with a start, slapping at her ankles.

They'd leave their horses tethered in the nearby hills, squirrel themselves silently away in that little cubbyhole of a cave she'd spied behind the butte, then walk out after the excitement had calmed down. They'd be at a disadvantage without the speed of the horses, but Harper horses weren't known for speed any way you looked at it. The six of them would just stay put till dark, is what they'd do. Walk out through the creek. They'd be almost invisible in the night. And with the night their horses couldn't be identified, either, should someone come sniffing around.

Lily smiled at the beauty of the plan, squashed a few more ants, and settled into a blissful sleep.

Rick brought by the newspaper Daddy had requested two nights after his trip to Fredericksburg, but it was a pure disappointment, schedule-wise. The only stagecoach it advertised was the one leaving three times a week from San Antonio to El Paso. And the fare was enough to frighten a person. Who had spending money enough to afford fifteen cents a mile just to traipse across a piece of desert? Lily couldn't recall laying eyes on more than a handful of real coins or bills her entire life. If they needed something for the ranch, Daddy just rounded up a cow and calf and headed off for the Henrys', or into Fredericksburg. A cow and calf were worth ten dollars hard currency, she'd always heard Daddy say.

Her sisters, however, didn't seem the least disappointed. They pawed through the paper till it was almost in shreds, admiring the advertisements from the different shops. March and April already had their money spent at Hartmann's Ladies Furnishings. They fairly salivated over the description of the dress goods, silks, shawls, hosiery, gloves, ribbons, and trimmings. May studied a notice for pianos with sheer covetousness, while June gazed longingly at the announcement of an evening of theater at the Casino Hall. Julie, of course, was after yarns and sewing notions. And then there was Daddy, poor Daddy, looking hungrily at the notices placed by the livestock dealers out of Abilene, Kansas.

Once it had gotten back into her hands, Lily went through the whole issue more carefully, but found only one item worthy of her further attention. It seems the Netty Apothecary had just received a shipment of Hungarian Leeches. Just what was a Hungarian Leech? And what would they want with them in Texas? Didn't Texas already have everything it needed?

Lily relinquished the paper once more to her sisters and set in to cooking up some hot chili for their supper, which she usually made when it was her turn to cook. She'd tried out some of Ooh-long's recipes once or twice on the family, but they hadn't taken to them. Now, as she chopped onions, she thought about the money situation again. Maybe people in San Antonio had hard cash to spend, but turning up with a pot full of gold right here in Gillespie County might have some effects they hadn't counted on. There were no two ways about it. If they got that money shipment, they'd none of them be able to spend it anywhere short of San Antonio. And they couldn't all pick up and just waltz off there, either. It would be mighty suspicious.

Lily sighed and ran out to the kitchen garden for some fresh red chile peppers. She kicked at the black ooze that kept creeping up around the plants no matter what Mama did to get rid of it. Disgusting, thick, sticky stuff. It sat around in flat, shiny-opaque puddles. It clumped on your boots something terrible, and was near impossible to get off. Wouldn't you know her daddy would pick just such a site to build his ranch on. Poor Daddy never did do the right thing.

It was Tom who unknowingly let the cat out of the bag. He'd been checking out the Henry herds just south and east of the Harper spread one afternoon, when the stage rumbled through on the nearby trail and lost a wheel practically under his nose. Tom, being the well-bred young man he was, moseyed over and gave the driver a hand. He reported the event that evening during his after-supper visit.

"It was Ned Brewster driving. He was keen to get back to San Antonio. He said he hadn't seen his wife in so long he was afraid she'd forget what he looked like. I met him once before at a barbecue most of the Henry hands went to this spring down in Boerne."

Rick looked over from his seat on the veranda rail. "Tall, heavyset fella, graying in the beard, with a big nose on the red side?"

"That describes him perfectly. He had a jug up alongside his seat."

"Must be to comfort him betwixt visits to his wife. Ned always appeared to like his tipple."

"Well," Tom continued, "he couldn't figure out why that particular wheel had chosen to bust off at that particular moment, but admitted he was relieved it happened today instead of next Tuesday, when he'll be heading out to the forts."

There was an unusual spark of interest in the females lounging around the porch. March pertly patted down her skirts, although they didn't need any rearrangement at the moment.

"I swan, Tom, you are a lucky young man to be working at a steady job at Mr. Henry's, 'stead of having to keep track of a stage and six huge horses while they traipse all over Texas."

"I don't know, March. There's a certain excitement to stagecoach driving, too. You get to see more of the land, and it could even be dangerous at times."

"Dangerous?" April's voice came out a high squeak. "I wouldn't want my man to be doing something dangerous. Though what could be dangerous about driving a coach evades me." She blinked at Rick as coquettishly as she knew how.

"Now, April dear, you needn't worry about such things. It's only the Injuns they've got to keep an eye out for. Texas is plumb civilized these days. Not like a few years back during the War. 'Twere desperadoes tucked up near every canyon in them days."

"Well, thank goodness they're gone. I'll bet you and the Confederate Army had a big hand in that."

Rick beamed, smoothed out his side whiskers, and started into a story about the good old days, but Tom interrupted.

"I hear enough of your rebel rousing back at Izzy's, Rick," he joshed. "It's time you got used to the fact that the War is over. But coaches, well, they might be something I'd like to give a try at before heading back East. Stagecoach driving, that is."

March's head banged on the veranda post she'd been leaning against. "Back East? You're seriously thinking about going back East, Tom?"

"Well, my parents have been patient with me thus far, but my one year 'educational leave' is almost up. Pop's got a post waiting for me at his bank back in Wilmington. Although," he considered, "although it seems to me I might be more comfortable taking on the supervision of his land and racing stock in the Brandywine after this. I've started to hint as much in

52

my letters home. Just to give him and Mother a chance to adjust to the idea."

Lily had been following the whole conversation, sprawled inelegantly over the wooden veranda steps. She felt for a possible splinter in her leg while her mind was teeming with the new information. Next Tuesday. This was Thursday. That gave them less than five days. Without horses, they'd have to wear the signs over their costumes, if they still wanted to disguise their true reasons for the robbery.

She finally rolled up her pant leg and located the errant splinter, ignoring the dirty looks from all five older sisters, whose ankles were chastely, and hotly, swathed in skirts.

Tom talking about going home had certainly taken March by surprise. Lily wondered if he really had the guts to cart a backcountry Texas girl home as his bride. If he didn't, March wouldn't be worth living with, no matter how you thought about it.

"When exactly is your time up, Tom?" she asked, trying to sound like it hardly mattered.

He grinned. "I wouldn't miss the cattle drive for anything. I already gave Mr. Henry notice it would be after that. He won't need to replace me till the spring, winters being as slow as they are around here. My parents gave me till my twenty-first birthday, and that's not till November."

"Be mighty dull without your evening visits, Tom."

"I didn't think you cared, Lily."

There was a round of laughter on her account, but Lily didn't rise to it. A lot of things could happen between now and autumn.

June broke the sudden lull. "There's still enough light. Let's play a game of pantomime!"

So they split into teams, using the veranda as a stage. The sisters were old hands at it, but gave deference to the young men's ideas. It was Rick's team that won, doing Robert E. Lee's surrender at Appomattox. Even without the gray beard, Rick managed to be serious and pitiful at the same time as General Lee, with April, Julie, and May as his staff, and June playing a sneering Grant to the hilt with her hair stuffed up under Lily's broad-brimmed hat. Lily personally thought that March's Pocahontas to Tom's Captain John Smith was more heartfelt, but Southern sympathies won the day. All the more reason to wear those signs of protest during the robbery.

The next morning the girls hauled their father into the stable and relayed to him their critical information. He listened to a summary of their robbery preparations thus far, then added a few words of wisdom. They were more practical than Lily had expected.

"First off, if you plan to use that little hidey-hole, you'd better lug up some water and provisions in advance of the event. Won't be no fun waitin' around for the coach through the hot part of the day without, nor the hiding after, either. Next, you'd better practice on keeping your traps shut for a good length of time." His eyes settled on each of his daughters in turn. "I know some few of you will be a mite high-strung in anticipation. It won't do to be chattering like wild birds. Sound travels over these open spaces." He scratched his sunburned pate. "Lastly, it might make some sense to have me awaitin' up in the hills with the horses. Iffen they took a mind to break loose and run home, you'd be left up the creek. High and dry."

Looking around at her sisters, Lily could tell that their one doubt was to have their daddy participate in any manner, howsoever small, in this endeavor. Like the kiss of death, it might be. Still, it sounded like an innocuous enough contribution. There was a silent vote between eyes, and March finally spoke.

"Fair enough, Daddy. We'll take up the water and provisions tomorrow, and you can keep a watch on the horses."

He nodded and walked out.

Then they had to get down to the signs. It wasn't easy coming up with paper big enough to catch anybody's attention. Julie had the brainstorm.

"Petticoats are white. So are sheets. We could trim some old ones into squares, so you couldn't tell, then paint onto them. Why, if I had time enough, I could even do the slogans up in stitchery!"

The thought seemed to please her mightily, but Lily squashed it fast. "And point the finger straight at us, Julie? Who else in these parts can stitch as finely and as fast as you?"

Julie accepted the compliment but was still put out. May solved the dilemma.

"Cut a hole in the middle, like Mexican ponchos. We'll just pull them over our heads, and it'll disguise us even better."

"Then when the deed is done, we need only pull them off, bundle them up, and burn them," added Lily.

They set to work.

It was lucky that Daddy had suggested the provisioning, after all, because when Lily escorted May and April out to the site the next day, they soon discovered that it was no mean feat to get up into the little cave in the rear side of the butte.

Lily sat inspecting the cave opening in frustration from atop Checkers. It was there all right, but just out of reach, even from horseback.

"We're going to need a ladder. A rope ladder. We'll have to set it up there, hanging down, then pull it in after us."

"Where are we going to get a rope ladder, Lily?" It was April, her voice rising higher than ever in despondency.

Lily sighed at the squeaky whine in her sister's voice. "Well, I guess we'll just have to go back and make one, won't we? We've still got almost three whole days."

They tucked the provisions out of sight behind a low rock and rode back, using the creek for practice.

• • •

Sunday morning, Lily hauled her sisters out of bed early, the lot of them protesting mightily, March the loudest.

"Is this really necessary, Lily?"

"Hush, you'll wake Mama. You know Daddy likes to let her sleep in on the Sabbath."

"He lets *all* of us sleep in on the Sabbath, Lily."

"Don't complain just 'cause you were sitting out till all hours with Tom last night. You knew there'd be work to do today."

"But there're only a few more months before he's intending to leave. And if he doesn't declare for me by then, I'll just fold up and die!"

"He ain't the last young man left in the world, you know. I thought you were set on playing the field in San Antonio."

"That was before." March was slowly pulling off her nightgown, blindly grasping for her chemise. April had already headed off for the line in front of the privy.

"And anyhow, you really believe he'll take you home to his high-and-mighty rich parents? He may call him 'Pop,' but sounds like his daddy's a straight-laced 'Father' to me. And he never calls his mama nothing but 'Mother.' I'll bet she's never dirtied her fingers in her life."

"Just because people live differently from us doesn't mean they're not people, Lily."

"That remains to be seen. April might have a chance with Rick, 'cause he's born and bred Texas, but if you ask me, Tom's just having some fun with you."

"I never asked you. Now clear out while I finish my toilette!"

"Toilette, my eyeballs." But Lily cleared out.

June was the tensest member of the group. It must've been something like the stage fright they say comes just before the curtain actually rises. Her hands kept fumbling the strands of rope the sisters were weaving together in the bunkhouse, so it was she they finally set as a lookout near the door. Her warbled warning came almost too late.

"Mama dear! You needn't step out on the Sabbath!"

Mama had stepped out anyway. The girls scrambled to sit on the ropes they were weaving and tried to shove the pot of paint they were readying behind them. They didn't make it with the paint.

"Whatever are you doing on the Lord's Day? Is that paint I see?"

Lily spoke up. "It's just a little surprise we were fixing for you, Mama. Thought we might paint the shutters on the house."

"In black?" Mama frowned. "Goodness knows they could use a sprucing, but black wouldn't be my first choice."

Lily sighed with relief. "Well then, as we aim to please you, why not tell us what color you'd really like?"

Mama stopped and thought. "My daddy took us all on a trip once, down south, way south and east of San Antonio. It was after the Mexican War was over, just before I met your daddy." She stopped again, her mind far away in remembrance.

"We took the wagon all the way to Corpus Christi, then sailed on a boat to Veracruz in Mexico. My daddy had some kind of a business deal he was involved in. I'm not sure if it even worked out. But Veracruz—it wasn't all brown and dry like everything I'd ever seen. It sat on the Gulf like a little jewel, and sea breezes wafted across the town . . . The adobes were white as the clouds in the sky, and had bright colors painted on the windows and shutters and doors. Every kind of blue, and yellow, green, and pink. I've never forgotten how wonderful it was." Her trance ended and she was back with her daughters again. "I don't think your daddy ever had any of those colors sitting in pots around here."

The girls were silent. No wonder Mama went for all those bright colors in dress cloth, Lily thought. No wonder she approved of Julie's stitching. Mama was plumb starved for color in her life. Yes sirree, if this thing worked out, Lily would personally paint up that ranch house like a Christmas tree.

"None of you seemed to be around"—Mama was talking again—"so I made up a cold bean salad for our dinner. You might as well come and eat it."

 Tuesday arrived at last. Lily was awake way before dawn, just lying in her bed. It was not that she was scared of the adventure to come. But what if something did go wrong? What if they were caught? It made her numb, that thought, from her knees right down to the tips of her toes. Once caught, they'd soon be discovered for what they really were—girls. A fine ending that would make to the Harper family.

Lily swung herself out of bed and hopped around to get rid of the numbness. Now her legs were all pins and needles, and that was almost worse. She stamped a foot. They wouldn't get caught. They just couldn't. She dressed up in her costume, which was not much different from her everyday outfit. The red bandanna she wound around her neck. Then she went to gather her sisters.

Mama had been told that her daughters had decided to take a picnic clear out to Enchanted Rock that day. She hadn't been enthusiastic about letting them go all that distance in the midst of the summer's heat, but Daddy had cut in at suppertime the night before.

"The girls been working hard for me lately, Gwen. And they been a little antsy, too. Could be a day off will calm 'em down some."

"If you really think so, Hy dear."

So it was done.

Now at daybreak, before Mama had even set foot out of her bed, the girls stood by the corral, mounts saddled and ready to go. Their daddy would follow them out later, to keep an eye on the horses at the tethering spot they'd agreed upon in the hills.

"Ready, sisters?" Lily said, smiling.

"No, you haven't got that quite right, Lily." It was June, building up her courage with a flourish. "Onward, Masked Avengers!"

The rest of them grinned, and they set out.

By the time they arrived at the butte, they already knew it was going to be another sizzling day. Their mounts were lathered up and panting for a drink, and the girls were not much better off. They used the horses to reach the little cave above the ground, hoisting Lily up with effort to fix the rope ladder. The supplies followed, May and June were sent up creek with the horses in tow, and the remainder settled behind the rocks to wait.

Lily had trouble sitting still and was soon prowling around. She'd forgotten something, she knew she had. Some teensy thing that might destroy them.

She scrambled up the rope ladder once to recheck the supplies, then paused to gulp hard at the water jug, and to splash some of the precious stuff over her face. She couldn't ever remember feeling this same-time dry, dusty cold and aguish hot when she was out working the herds.

Walking to the road, she stopped short as she focused on

the shallow stream that bisected it at the bottom of the hill. Of course! They needed to set up a false trail to confuse the enemy.

Lily raced back, corralled April and Julie, and with them walked directly into the stream across the road, before retracing their steps backward to the butte.

"And what was all that in favor of?" March asked, dabbing delicately at her temples with Mama's embroidered handkerchief. Real *ladies* didn't sweat, after all.

"It was in favor of us all getting away clean and scot-free. It makes it seem like we took off to the east, 'stead of to the west, like we're planning on doing. Now, nobody budge!"

"If you say so. Though I really think you're playing this all out of proportion . . ."

March could get so tedious at times.

After a spell, May and June came hobbling into view down the creek after hiding the horses. From their sways and groans they looked like two very young cowpokes that'd butted up against some of the Harper family's moonshine unawares, but they were only wretchedly uncomfortable in Daddy's old boots, and needing water. The canteen they'd kept out of the cave was passed around once, but the noon sun parched them as soon as they'd swallowed.

With a look at the shimmering sky, March bit the bullet first. "It's time for the ponchos, sisters."

"No," moaned Julie.

"It'll make us even hotter!"

"May . . . Now."

They did it. April had on the **DOWN WITH U. S. GRANT!** offering, and May and Lily had to share the **REBELLION TO TYRANTS** slogan, because they'd found it too long to letter boldly on just one poncho. Lily got the **IS OBEDIENCE TO GOD** half, which meant she and May would have to stand next to each other during the holdup, or the words wouldn't make a whole lot of sense.

Lily was still smoothing the white cloth down over her shirt front, trying to read the words backward and upside down to see if they were really effectively placed, when the first sign of the stagecoach appeared.

It was a light plume of dust rising above the hill to the south. Next, ever so distantly, they heard the sound of hoofbeats. May was apple-green, and Julie was hugging her stomach. "I don't think I feel very well—" Julie disappeared from sight.

"Told her not to eat much this morning," Lily muttered as she rounded a corner of rock, rifle hugged to her body. "Now she's going to upchuck it all and leave the work to us."

The hoofbeats were coming closer, and they could hear wagon wheels rattling over the uneven ground. The stage was certainly in a hurry.

March took over again. "Julie, get back here! Take your position like you promised! With April, to the left. May and Lily, to the right. June, you and I are going to face down that stage in the middle of the road."

Lily was quite taken by March's sudden decisiveness. Apparently the others were as well, and they ran to do her bidding, just in time. They could hear the horses struggling up the far incline. The Harper girls shoved down their hats, pulled up their bandannas, and readied their guns in determined poses. The stagecoach came on.

Lily remembered it later almost like it was a dream. An endlessly slow dream. The hooves of the lead pair were rising and falling into the dry earth of the road. Lily had never looked at a galloping horse from quite this perspective, and the power in the motion was impressive. It was also relentless, like the cogs in Daddy's eight-day clock over the mantel: once wound, they just kept turning. The horses would never stop. They would plow right through the lot of them, crushing them into the dust. Another pair followed, and yet another, backed up by the stagecoach itself.

The coach lumbered over the rise and began the slide down. There was the dust-covered driver, reins tightly in hand, his red nose glowing in the sun's rays. There was his jug, snuggled up far too close to his body. It was so close because there was a second rider sitting on the driver's seat. And the second man was riding shotgun.

"Halt!"

March's shout, audible above the creaking coach and laboring horses, broke the spell, at least for Lily. She found herself cocking her rifle, legs spread wide, standing firm, May equally firm to one side. A quick glance at March and June showed they stood amazingly still, dead center in the road, just like March had claimed they would. Even April and Julie acted like they meant business. Lily felt a rush of pride as reins were pulled and a long, frantic "Whoa!" was called out. The horses stopped, panting and frothing at the mouth, the first pair not more than six inches before March.

"Stand and deliver!"

They'd talked quite a bit about the proper phrases to use at this point of the operation. June had been all for "Your money or your life!" but Lily had pointed out that that particular phrase might be a little too antagonistic, seeing as how they really didn't intend to take any lives.

"Stand and deliver!" seemed to do the trick. The guard lowered his shotgun, and four passengers popped their heads out of the windows of the coach, two on either side. They were all bearded, and the farthest one out had epaulets on his shoulders. Probably they were officers, maybe even the paymaster, bound for the forts. Good. They all ought to be able to read the signs well enough.

March aimed her rifle at the guard. "Drop it!"

There was a soft thud as his shotgun hit the dirt. But Ned was still sitting there, looking like he needed a quick pull from the jug.

"The money box!" snarled March. "And quickly, Yankee pawn!"

"I ain't no Yankee," Ned complained. "Born and bred in Texas, I be. Fought with the South like any true Texan."

Lily felt a gesture needed to be made at this point to move things along, before the men in the coach decided for action. She aimed casually and put a hole clean through Ned's jug. It was a nice shot, square on. The driver watched the whiskey flowing out and near cried. Then he got up and unbuckled the straps holding down the strongbox on the coach roof behind him.

"Throw it down!"

It landed with a thud.

"The other luggage, too."

"That be private property!"

March aimed her gun more pointedly. "Do it!"

He did it.

"Now move that coach, and don't stop this side of the territories!"

Ned took the reins in his hands, gave another sorrowful look at his demolished jug, and finally shook the reins. The horses seemed more inclined to prolong their unexpected rest. March motioned June out of the right-of-way and shot her rifle off into the sky. The other Harpers followed suit. The team jumped, skittered, then set off at a gallop.

"Quickly now, all of you," prodded March, "help get these things out of sight before they come to their senses and head back for us."

The strongbox was heavier than anyone had anticipated, but the girls carried it with goodwill to just beneath the cave. The heavier it was, the more gold it must contain, after all. Then they went back for the odds and ends belonging to the passengers. There was one traveling trunk, and three large carpetbags. In short order, everything but the two heavy boxes

63

was stashed in the cave. The girls stood staring at these, knowing they were too unwieldy to hoist up.

"How are we ever going to drag these up to the hills?" wailed Julie. "We hardly got them out of the road!"

"Never fear." Lily scrambled up the rope ladder and came back down with a small ax and a saddlebag. "If you're going to do a job, do it right."

"Maybe there's something to your practical streak after all, Lily," March said.

"Thank you, big sister. I sure did admire your handling of the situation back there. You were plumb convincing."

March pulled off her hat, releasing her long golden tresses to fan down over her shoulders. "I do believe stressful situations bring out the best in me."

"Daddy would've been proud," said April.

"Maybe even Mama, sort of," Lily added.

"Enough of this lollygagging and congratulating." May was getting impatient. "I just now decided how I'm going to spend my share. Let's get it opened!"

Lily stopped, the ax poised in the air. "How, May?"

"I'm going to buy the biggest, finest piano in Texas, that's what."

Lily's ax arm slowly descended. "You think the whole county won't notice that kind of opulence, May? We've got to go easy on this, you know. Show our hand like that, and it'll be curtains for us."

"Oh, pooh, Lily," interrupted June. "Just get the box opened."

Lily knew there'd be trouble coming from this, she felt it in her bones. But she struck at the lock nevertheless, again and again. One thing could be said for those Yankees, right enough. They knew how to make a strong lock.

Finally it sprung. The Harper girls crowded around, but March pushed them all aside. "I'm the oldest. I shall open it."

She took a deep breath and slowly raised the top. Then

64

it was open and they were all staring down into the box. Lily reacted first. She laughed. Then she laughed harder, until her stomach began to pain.

"It ain't gold at all! It's currency! Almost worthless currency! Those poor Yankee soldiers must be worse off than we are!"

March and April rifled through the depth of the strongbox. It was so. Just neat stacks of greenbacks. Greenbacks that would have to be converted to coin before they were spent, and at the local conversion rate of nearly fifty cents lost to the dollar. If anyone could be found willing to make the exchange, which was highly unlikely.

"Damnation!"

Five Harper girls edged back and gaped at March.

"Why, March dear, such a thing to come from your mouth." Julie was shocked to the core.

"Damn all Yankees!" March ripped off her sign that read **YANKEES, GO HOME!** and stomped it into the dust. Her kerchief came with it as she stood there glaring, her hair shimmering in the sun.

"Even sweet Tom Carter?" tested May.

"He's a Yankee, too, isn't he? And he's set to go off and leave me in this no-good, dried-out desolation of a place."

"How could you speak so of your birthplace, March Harper?"

March turned on April. "Just because you've almost landed a genuine Southerner, don't go using that sweetness-and-light tone of yours on me, sister. Rick with his sad face and memories of glory lost. I'll have none of that. It's future glories I'm after. And I don't guess I'll ever find them in this hellhole full of dying cattle and lost dreams!"

"March, maybe we ought to try out the trunk? You never can tell—"

"Back off, Lily. You only did this for a lark, anyway. You're the only one who had nothing to gain from this piece of larceny. You're the only one besides Daddy who can stand the Double H and everything it means!"

Such recriminations could have gone on into the night if May's finely tuned ears hadn't picked up a distant noise. "Sisters, please. I think I hear a horse!"

They stood like statues for a split second, then Lily bent to stuff the almost useless currency into a saddlebag. The rest scampered for the rope ladder. With a few bills still scattered in the dust, Lily doubled over once more to pick up March's soiled poncho and followed them up, pulling the ladder after her. She scrunched herself into the cramped confines of the low cave just as hoofbeats rounded the butte. Lily desperately wanted to peek over the edge, but instead made herself as flat and small as humanly possible, and concentrated on listening.

The horses ground to a halt by the strongbox and trunk just below.

"This looks like the spot, Captain Barnes, sir."

"It does, lieutenant. But where the devil have they gotten off to? They can't have disappeared into thin air. It took us but a few moments to free these horses from harness. Is there a trail of hoofprints?"

There was silence while the lieutenant apparently surveyed the scene from a farther distance, then the sound of his returning mount.

"Nothing like that, sir. But there are a few boot tracks making into the creek across the road. It just don't make sense, their disappearing like this."

"And I didn't care for the impertinence of the assault, either. 'Yankees, Go Home!' indeed. I'd much prefer a good, honest desperado do the deed. When I arrived from headquarters in Washington last month, I was told the rebels in Texas were no longer a threat."

"By whom, sir? I've been around longer. They've been holding Klan meetings on the desert fifteen miles outside of San Antonio for nearly a year now."

"And the provisional government hasn't stopped them?"

"They're hard, sir, they are. These rebels throw our laws

66

right back at us. They just laugh in our faces and tell us the Bill of Rights of the glorious Union guarantees every free man the right to gather in assembly." He stopped. "Think the Klan could be behind this?"

"I've seen what they've done in the Carolinas. It's entirely possible, Lieutenant Corcoran, entirely possible. Those devils have a way of turning invisible whenever they want."

Lily could hear the horses wheeling around under their riders.

"Let's get back to the stage and on to McKavett to make a report."

"What about your wife's trunk, sir?"

"Tie that rope around it and we'll have a go at dragging it back. It's too heavy to carry. And she'll have my head, right enough, if I turn up without it. Her mother's silver tea set is inside, wrapped up in gowns. I told her this was not the post to be lugging all those fripperies out to. You'd think after fifteen years as an officer's wife she'd take on some common sense."

"Yes, sir. And should the civilian authorities be contacted?"

"We'll send a message down to Fredericksburg. That's the biggest town hereabouts, isn't it?"

"Yes, sir, outside of San Antonio."

"It might be the best we can do. Too bad about the money, though. The enlisted men at Mason and McKavett haven't been paid in close to eight months. Now it'll be another few. They'll be hell to keep in order."

"And the desertion rate will go up again."

"I can hardly blame them. Who would want to live in this godforsaken country?"

"This is still the Hill Country, sir, or at least the final edge of it. Wait till you see the true desert."

"It gets worse?"

Lily couldn't hear the lieutenant's reply. He'd apparently

done his piece of the work, and the officers were off around the butte and up the trail again.

"What's the Klan?"

Lily thought it was Julie's whispered voice she detected in the silence following the Army officers' departure. Surprisingly, April answered.

"Rick told me about them. The Ku Klux Klan. It's a fraternal order of brotherhood, made up of old officers and such like from the Confederacy days. Rick says they dress up in white sheets and try to right the wrongs done by the carpetbaggers."

June was astounded. "Our slogans were on white, and they looked like sheets, pulled over our heads like that. Why, we were part of a play we didn't even know anything about!"

May changed the subject. "We should've opened that trunk first. It was filled with silver, and lovely gowns."

"Lay off, May. You turn your nose up at March's hand-me-downs. You were planning on maybe wearing the stolen dresses of a Yankee officer's wife? How would you explain that to Mama?"

"Just because you haven't grown up enough to want to step into a gown yet, Lily Harper—"

"Enough!" March barked. "I want nothing but silence till we see the sun setting."

Julie started to whimper.

"What is it now?"

"Couldn't we even have some water first?"

The leather bag was passed around and silence descended.

Lily woke from a long, disoriented doze, clothes stuck to her body from the humid tightness of the place. Closest to the cave's opening, she peered out. Not only had the sun set but it was almost dark. She gave a few tentative nudges with her boots and heard the moans of protest.

"Stop it, Lily. It can't be morning yet."

"No, it surely isn't. It's almost black night. And Daddy's probably worried to distraction in the hills."

"What?"

"It couldn't be."

"I had no intention of drifting off like that."

Then, muscles cramped and groaning, the Harper girls lowered themselves and their questionable loot from their aerie. It was a long, slow hike through the creek into the hills. Their daddy was waiting, and if it'd been light enough, Lily would probably have been able to vouch that he had fewer hairs than ever on his head.

In all their frantic making of plans, the girls had forgotten one thing. Two things, actually. After dumping the guns, loot, and costumes in Dead Man's Canyon on the way back, they rode into the ranch demurely enough to suit anyone. Anyone except Tom and Rick. The two suitors were wearing down a path in front of the veranda, Tom studiously copying Rick's bowlegged stride. A flustered Mama stood close by. The young men strode up to the girls and helped March and April to dismount.

"Where've you been? We've nearly gone crazy for the past three hours!"

"Why, Tom, you were worried about me!"

Rick was brusquer. "Get down here, April! How'd you ever

get such a fool notion in your head? Didn't you know there's Indians out there? You wanted an excursion, you could've waited till Sunday for Tom and me to escort the lot of you!"

"Ain't neither of them married to you two," pointed out Lily. "I don't see why they have to account for every blessed minute. Not yet. We had a good day. It just took longer to get there and back than we anticipated. We didn't figure on anybody being worried, not until we bumped into Daddy on the way back. Then we hightailed it home fast as we could." She stopped. "You want to do something useful, you can help cool off the horses. It might cool you down some, too."

"Lily! How dare you speak so!" Mama scolded.

"Sorry, Mama. I wouldn't have you worried for the world. I just don't like my big sisters looked on as property, is all."

"You watch your tongue, young lady."

"Aw, Mama." Lily jumped off her horse and ran to give her mother a hug. "It did us a plumb lot of good being off on our own for a bit like we did. Didn't you ever have a lark when you were young?"

Her mama's body softened and began to hug back. "Well, I guess maybe I did, once or twice, at that." Then her arms slipped away. "Go take care of your horse, then get directly to bed, young lady. That goes for the rest of you, as well." She looked toward her husband to take over from there.

"You fellas better be heading back to Izzy's place. Enough excitement for one night as it is. Much obliged to you for setting with the missus and keeping her company like you done."

The whole Harper family had a late start the next morning. And when the girls finally finished their chores and gathered in the canyon after their noon meal, the excitement of the previous day had worn off. They were all of them feeling the letdown.

May kicked at the saddlebags that held the currency. "We

70

might as well burn the stuff. That's how much good it'll do us. There won't be any piano out of that."

But June was studying the carpetbags. "Doesn't anyone want to see what's inside these? There're three of them, after all."

"And all belonging to Yankee officers," said April, with a sniff.

"The more reason to find out what's inside," argued Lily.

"All right, then." March took charge again. "Let's see what we can save from our latest debacle."

The first bag was opened.

"Linens," wailed Julie. "Yankee linens! And not too clean, either." She pulled the stuff out for display. It was true. Shirts, several soiled white gloves, a union suit, one pair of blue woolen trousers, and assorted socks. She burrowed to the bottom and fetched out all that remained: a packet of letters, carefully tied up in a ribbon, and a large, smoothly polished wooden box.

Lily slipped the clasp and opened it.

"Oh, pooh. More guns!" Julie exclaimed.

But Lily was still examining the contents carefully. "Not just guns, sister. Matched dueling pistols. Daddy told me about such. I'm sure he'd admire to add these to his collection."

"To display on the mantel?" March asked.

Lily sank back on her haunches. "Well, I guess it's maybe true, after all."

"What?"

"What they say about no good ever coming out of doing wrong. Here we went to all that trouble, and what have we got to show for it? Dirty Yankee linens, and a pair of dueling pistols that won't do any of us any good. I guess the Harper luck struck again."

"There are still the other bags. What about them?"

"Check if you want, June." Lily threw up her hands. "The rest of this stuff we'll just have to bury and take our chances.

Things being as dry as they are out here, it'd be just our luck to set the hills alight if we tried burning it."

Apparently unwilling to give up just yet, June attacked the remainder of their loot. There was more clothing, some items cleaner than others. There were a few more letters, one Bible, a set of silver spurs, ten dollars in currency, and one five-dollar gold piece. They sat looking at the five-dollar gold piece.

"Do you suppose Daddy can save the ranch with that, Miss Lily?"

"You know he can't, March."

"Couldn't we try to forget it ever happened? I think I'd like to go back home and work on my sampler."

"Just see that your next one reads 'Crime Does Not Pay,' Julie."

"Look who's becoming almighty moral all of a sudden."

"Hush up, March. Let's just get the funeral over with."

Lily was glad her daddy was taking it so nice. Considering as how the results hadn't amounted to much. After disposing of the evidence, they'd taken him the currency, along with the spurs, pistols, and gold piece. He'd inspected the sum total of loot displayed there on his workbench in the stable, then shrugged.

"I guess you done as good as could be expected. It just weren't meant to be. I just wonder when something *is* meant to be, that's all."

Then he'd smiled a little before rubbing his stomach. "No sense in crying over spilt milk, is there?"

"Indigestion bothering you again, Daddy?" Lily asked.

"It seems to be getting worse and worse these last few months."

"It must be an awful thing to be plagued with something like that, a man who loves his food like you do."

"I don't guess you'll ever inherit that, Lily, events sliding off your back the way they do."

Then all the girls were huddling around Daddy, patting, hugging, comforting him.

His smile turned brighter. "Well, I reckon a flock of sons couldn't be as much a comfort to a man as you daughters are sometimes. Nor try harder. I'll just have to do some more thinking, like you said. As for this stuff"—he waved at their loot—"why don't I just tuck it away for a spell. You never can tell when greenbacks may come back into style in Texas."

12

Word traveled slowly around the county, but not that slowly. The next night, Tom and Rick were back, having forgiven all in their excitement to pass on the news that had come to the Henry ranch that day. The whole family sat out on the veranda, finishing off the custard the girls had cobbled together, Daddy strumming his guitar plaintively in the background from his rocker.

"I told you stagecoach driving could be dangerous, Tom. I surely hope you never mean to try it out now!"

March gazed into his eyes for a moment, then spoiled the effect by adding, "And then what happened?"

"There were desperadoes all over, maybe a dozen of them!"

"Ned only counted but six, Tom."

"Come on, Rick, what about behind the butte? Could've been more hiding there, as backup, couldn't there?"

"Maybe so, maybe not. It's pretty hard to get up that many

men in the middle of the day out here. Unless they come up from Fredericksburg, or down from the forts themselves."

"That'd be an idea!"

Tom's eyes were shiny bright with the romance of it. That's why he'd come out West, after all. And to think he'd been talking to Ned Brewster little more than a week before. "A regiment could have come down from McKavett and plundered their own payroll!"

"It's clear you ain't ever been part of the military, Tom," interrupted Rick, wiping a bit of custard from his muttonchops. "They hardly got a whole regiment holding down any one of them frontier forts. And the commanding officers keep their men occupied every solitary moment—to keep 'em from getting into mischief like this. Why, they've got roll call maybe six times a day. There's no way a dozen or even six men could disappear like that."

"How about deserters?" Daddy spoke up. "I hear the desertion rate is something fierce for the Yankees out here. It could account for the words you was mentioning being displayed."

"I just don't know what's coming to the world anymore." Mama was speaking placidly as usual, but with the old worry line on her brow. "Young people don't seem to want to do things the hard way."

"And it was a wonder no one was killed. Why, we heard that Ned was just an inch from death. It was his whiskey jug that saved him."

Lily giggled. Ned had never been anywhere near to death, not with her shooting.

Daddy's strumming finger stopped in the middle of a chord. "What's so funny, Lily? That a fine, God-fearing man was saved for his family?"

"Course not, Daddy. From what I hear, though, I just bet Ned Brewster was more upset about his lost whiskey than the payroll."

"Into the house, young lady! To think that a daughter of mine should even mention the Devil's Brew in my hearing. Is that how I raised you?"

"No, Daddy. Sorry, Mama." Daddy sure could pull off that innocent act of his with authority. "Night, all."

She went inside obediently, but sat herself down directly next to the open door, leaning up against the inside wall. There was no way she'd miss hearing the rest.

"Funny thing, though."

"What's that, Rick?"

"Why, April, this all happened Tuesday, same day you girls went off to Enchanted Rock. You didn't see anything suspicious, did you?"

"Rick dear, it was so hot even the rattlesnakes were hiding. 'Sides, how would you expect me to notice something suspicious? I've never been anywhere to know what suspicious is."

"Well, I thought as much. You might be getting a visit from the sheriff anyhow."

Daddy was tensing, his ears pricking up. "Sheriff?"

"O. T. Williams, out of Fredericksburg. Seeing as how it happened in Gillespie County, his jurisdiction. He don't seem too upset, though. It kind of tickled him it might be the Klan paying the Yankees back some."

"That what folks is saying?"

"On the whole, Mr. Harper, sir. It kind of gave us all a lift, it did."

"If that's the case, maybe it'll all turn out all right anyway."

The sheriff turned up first thing the next morning. As Daddy said later, he either flew over from Fredericksburg, or camped out on their land the night before, in preparation. Lily figured on the camping part.

He was not a tall man, this Williams; rather thick, disheveled, and unshaven. They hollered him in the front door as they were finishing their breakfast, and he waved them back into their seats to polish off their plates as he walked around the big table, hat politely in hand, spurs clinking, gun belt with its matching revolvers slung low over his tight paunch.

Finally he stopped his prowling to run a hand through his lank, dust-streaked brown hair and read Julie's handiwork. "It's good to find a family who still abides by Christian values."

Daddy sprang up now, pulling his suspenders over the top of his red union suit.

"How can we help you, neighbor? Maybe my girls can rustle up some eggs for you?"

"Et on the road." Broad fingers pulled at the shiny copper badge that hung from his plaid shirt, right over the heart. "O. T. Williams, sheriff of the county."

Daddy extended his hand to shake. "Seems like I've seen you once or twice down to Fredericksburg."

"Likely have. I don't usually stray this far from home. Don't usually have need to. I suppose you've heard what brings me round now."

Daddy scratched his head. "Might could be that piece of business with the stagecoach folks been talking about."

"The same. The way I figure it, the perpetrators had to go either east or west. I would have known if something was brewing south, towards town. And there ain't hardly nothing to go to, north." He paused, eyeing Daddy. "I hear tell your daughters were off that way the same day. Thought maybe they could cast some light on the situation."

Daddy turned around to the table. "Anything to say for yourselves?"

The six Harper girls sat stone still. Mama was confused. "What could my daughters possibly know about desperadoes?"

Williams nodded his head toward her. "I don't mean to upset you none, ma'am. It just seems to me if they was on their way to Enchanted Rock like some of Henry's boys said, they'd of been crossing the stage road about the right time. They might of seen some horses, or maybe even heard something—"

Lily caught dangerously guilty expressions beginning to crowd across her sisters' faces. She let go of the black braid that had found its way into her hand. "Well, there might have been something . . ."

"Yes, young lady?"

"After you get off our land, and cross the road . . ."

"Yes?"

"Past where the creek, Threadgills it would be, turns to meet up with Hickory?"

"Well?"

"Saw some hoofprints round about there, heading up towards the German Settlements. I don't know how old they were, though, on account of it's been so dry the land is like paper with a pencil took to it. Everything gets marked up."

"That's all?"

"Yes, sir."

"Were they shod?"

Lily brushed the dark bangs off her forehead with one hand while tugging again at her braid with the other. "You mean there might be Apache nearby, and all of us waltzing around the countryside by ourselves like Eastern touristers?"

"Not to worry, little girl." He turned to Daddy. "But I'd keep a tight rein on your offspring till we get this cleared up. It might just of been a one-time lark, to put a little fear of the Texans into them Yankees. Then again, there's no saying it wasn't a true band of desperadoes using Texan sympathies to cover their baser natures."

"It's too bad old Sam Houston ain't still around," Daddy broke in. "Him and his Rangers sure knew how to keep law and order around these parts."

"If Sam Houston hadn't of kicked off during the War, we would of been bigger by half of Mexico by now."

"Pity the good die young."

"He was near seventy, if he was a day, Mr. Harper."

"Hy, call me Hy. And he still had the strength of his mind,

even if it did weaken a mite there for a while in the direction of the North."

"Principles is principles, Hy. You can't begrudge Houston that. He come around to the South after a while." The sheriff stopped and acted like he was about to spit, realizing he was inside a house in the nick of time. He adjusted his gun belt instead. "Well now, this conversation don't seem to be getting us any further in the right direction. I guess I better head off and check those hoofprints." He inclined his big head toward the table. "Good day to you, Mrs. Harper, and to all your lovely daughters, too. Six of them, and all looking as fit and fair as the day is long. Ain't that some blessing!"

Williams moved to go, then halted to fish a flimsy piece of cloth from his breast pocket.

"By the bye, any of you recognize the initials on this?"

He dropped the cloth onto the breakfast table. It lit on the empty biscuit platter, right in front of Mama. She squinted slightly to make out the lettering.

"Why, those are my maiden initials, Mr. Williams. *G.W.*, for Gwendolyn Winslow. And I remember that lace, too. I stitched it around myself, when I was no older than my girls." Her head rose. "It seems to me I gave this to you, March."

March's nose quivered ever so perceptibly. "You did at that, Mama. I lost it out on the range some time ago and hadn't the heart to mention it to you."

Mama looked up at the sheriff. "It's very kind of you to take the trouble to return it to us, sir. Good Irish linen is almost impossible to come by these days."

"O.T., ma'am. I'm generally known as O.T. And I'm pleased to return it to its rightful owner. It was just sitting out there for the picking on my way to your ranch this morning."

He nodded pleasantly again, and this time when he turned, the sheriff actually left.

Williams had barely gotten off the veranda, slapped his hat back on his head, and mounted his waiting horse before Daddy had his own handkerchief out, mopping his face.

"Why, Hy dear, you're all flushed. You wouldn't be coming down with one of your malarial spells, I hope."

"Just the heat, Gwendolyn. It feels like it's fixing to be an unusually hot day."

Lily's elbow prodded at her nearest sister. "A good reason to get a head start on the chores. Daddy's hardly ever wrong about the weather."

13

☞ Lily rode up to Dead Man's Canyon that afternoon. Just on a hunch, to be sure they'd covered up every last sign from the holdup. Not that anyone had been known to wander around back there. It was Harper land, after all.

She paused at the entrance to the canyon to rest her horse, then found her eyes wandering around the scrappy ground. It was so dry it had gone from the rock-hard stage to crumbling into mounds of sand if you so much as touched it. That tall tale she'd told the sheriff. It could be true, after all. There hadn't been any rain in over six months, and even the stream they'd used to cool down the whiskey had since dried up. The signs of the Harpers' frequent comings and goings in this direction were plentiful.

She pressed her horse on, past the demolished still, then headed for the stunted juniper near the base of the western cliff where they'd buried the carpetbags and what everyone now thought of as their Klan outfits.

The dry dust under the cliff seemed to be in more disarray

than it ought. Lily got off the horse. It hadn't seemed necessary to bury the stuff that deeply. And besides, the ground under the upper layer of dust and sand had been like granite and too hard to work any more than a couple of feet.

The stones she'd set on top looked different as well, like they'd maybe been picked up and set down again. Lily prodded the spot with her boot, then got on her knees and frantically began pawing. The gritty dirt bit into her hands and broke her fingernails. She didn't pay any attention, just kept burrowing. Finally, she gave up and ran over to Checkers, then galloped like a demon back to the ranch. The carpetbags were gone. The disguises were gone. What in tarnation had happened?

It took a while to collect Daddy and the girls. March and April had been in the cool of the house, busy with Mama and the dresses, as usual. Lily barged in and tried to give them a signal. They blissfully ignored her.

"If my ship ever comes in, Mama, I'm going to get you a genuine Singer sewing machine," March was saying.

Mama removed a pin from her mouth. "What a sweet thought, dear. With some cloth to run through it, there's no end to what we could create between us. Julie has a fine hand, but you've a better eye for design."

"We'll need subscriptions to *Godey's Lady's Book* and *Peterson's*, too," added April. "These old ones from Mrs. Henry are from before the War, for heaven's sake. Who knows what they're wearing in Paris or New York this season?"

"And who cares?" Lily wasn't going to wait. "Excuse me, all, but Daddy has a sudden need for you. Not you, Mama, just the girls."

"But we've done our chores, Lily," April said.

They were still giving her a hard time, smug in their belief that they were beyond discovery. She came up with another tall tale. "I think he's been reconsidering the Longhorn business. He might want to plot out a possible strategy to round some up."

"Well, why does he need March and me for that, Lily? You're the expert on stock. Figure it out, and we'll talk to you later. I've already had too much sun on me today. I declare, my complexion's gotten so brown Rick's going to think I'm part Apache."

March peeked into the grainy mirror hanging over an old oak dresser by her bed. She patted back some fine blond strands and grimaced. "Mine, too."

"March . . . April . . . Daddy said *now*."

They sighed, but finally followed her out of the bedroom and down the narrow hall to the living area of the ranch house. Lily heard May trilling in the kitchen and collared her as well. June and Julie were waiting on the veranda.

"Where is Daddy?" June asked. "He's not out at the stable like you said, Lily."

"Wherever he is, we've got to find him fast. There's trouble. With a capital 'T.' "

Daddy listened to Lily's recitation in silence, ominous rumblings from his stomach the only sign of his distress. "You figure they can pin anything on you from what was buried up there?"

"The Klan outfits. That is, the signs . . ."

"Yes, Lily?"

"Well, they were made from old petticoats."

Daddy groaned. "I suppose they even had some lace on them?"

"Not a lot," said March. "We saved as much as we could. Lace is too dear to throw away like that, you know."

"With us always economizing," added April.

"Admirable."

"It wasn't really fine lawn cloth, Daddy. In fact, it could be mistaken for bed linens. Maybe."

"That's some consolation, Julie. Some, but not enough. And I've been meaning to ask you something, too, March."

"Yes, Daddy?"

"About your mama's handkerchief. Exactly how long you been missing it?"

March turned whiter than at the breakfast table that morning. "Since last Tuesday. Since the robbery. I know I had it there, but—"

Daddy was at the complete end of his tether. "I wish to high heaven we *had* been meeting about Longhorns. I don't figure I'll ever be able to hang on to the Double H from a jail cell —or worse."

"What are you going on about, Daddy?"

"You're in the clear."

"We wouldn't ever tell on you, Daddy!"

"You think I'd really wash my hands of the lot of you and send you off to prison? Nope. A father's duty is to protect his youngsters, and I guess I know my duty."

Daddy surely was distressed, but it was nice to have him stand by them all like this. Lily reached out and gave him a hug. He shoved her off, not unkindly, and finished his piece.

"When O. T. Williams turns up again, and you can be sure he will, I'll just have to take full responsibility. You girls will have to back me up. Swear I forced you into the whole thing. That'll get you off, at least."

Julie started in to snivel. "I don't want to see you strung up, Daddy! Who'd take care of Mama and us?"

"We can't let you do it, Daddy!" Lily blurted out. "The rest of us might be able to pull through, but without you, Mama would just fold up and wilt away."

Her words were digested, then March moved to stand beside Daddy, facing the rest of them. "Julie and Lily are right, and the rest of you know it. The stagecoach may have been Daddy's idea, but we acted on that idea, and it's our responsibility. Totally. If Mr. O. T. Williams comes around again, I expect us Harper girls to stand together. Mama needs Daddy to take care of her, and if any of you even consider implicating Daddy in any of this, I'll, I'll—" She paused, considering. "I'll pull out your hair till you're balder than poor Daddy!"

Five heads bowed down before March and Daddy, Julie clutching her snooded bun in terror. It was perfectly clear. If trouble came, they took the brunt of it. Perhaps they'd get some leniency for their youth.

"We ought to go on back to the house and pull out the family Bible," May murmured at last. "Maybe sing a few hymns. We're not in Daddy's hands anymore, and a little inspiration wouldn't hurt."

14

The sheriff turned up again just before sundown, with a posse of about ten men. Lily couldn't figure why he'd brought so many. Did he think the Harpers would go violent on him? They were just six young ladies, after all.

The whole family was clustered around the veranda with Tom and Rick. Everything went silent when the first sound of hoofbeats came up the valley.

"Expecting company, Mr. Harper?"

Daddy and Mama were enthroned on the two rocking chairs, Mama's bent slightly toward Daddy's, so she could keep him cool with her fan.

"Can't say that I am, aside from those present, of course. There do seem to be a lot of horses, coming on apace."

The Harper girls followed their daddy's lead. They just sat there and waited for the riders to arrive. Lily was propped up against the ranch-house wall, her feet stretched out next to

Daddy's chair, where she could hear the near-hysterical rumblings of his stomach.

Herself, she felt as composed as was possible. They'd taken their chances like they'd been obligated to. It wasn't from trying that the ranch was still unsaved. There wasn't anything left to be done, so there wasn't much point in getting further upset.

As the horses roared nearer, though, she noticed subtle changes in her sisters. March and April were pale. So pale, you would never have guessed they'd been worrying over their complexions earlier. May had been humming softly to herself from her seat on the steps just before the approach; now she was silent. June had straightened up and taken on the guise of a Christian martyr about to face the lions, while, next to her, Julie's fingers had stopped their stitching and were poised in midair, trembling slightly.

The riders pulled up in a haze of dust in front of the veranda. There was much dismounting and embarrassed shuffling before Sheriff O. T. Williams presented himself. This time, he didn't bother to remove his hat. He strode up to Daddy, who hadn't yet gotten out of his rocking chair. Lily figured he was scared his knees wouldn't support him.

"Sorry to have to do this, Harper, but as we was saying earlier, principles is principles."

"What's troubling your mind, O.T.?"

"Gonna have to arrest the lot of you, is what."

Tom, startled, tightened the arm he'd had draped around March. Rick jumped up, fists clenched and whiskers bristling. April put a hand on his shoulder to hold him back from the sheriff. Daddy finally pried himself out of the chair. His legs held.

"I don't think I understand your meaning, sir."

"My meaning is clear, as I intend to be. I arrest you, Hy Harper, your wife, and daughters, for robbing the stagecoach last Tuesday, with malice aforethought." He added, almost as an afterthought, "In the name of the Law."

84

Lily watched Mama blink. "Whatever is all this about, Hy?"

"I'm sure *I* don't know, Gwendolyn. I do think it's a fine state of affairs, though, when a man can't even rest on his veranda and play a little music after a hard day's work, without getting accosted by the Law. I thought we Texans still had some rights, even back under the Union."

"Don't you pull that plumb-innocent act on me, Hy Harper. I know what I know, and I found what I found. That handkerchief down by the butte where the robbery took place, for one. It was right inside that little cave where you all must of hid out after the act. And the leftovers from the robbery up in your own canyon, on your own land. Petticoats!" His still-unshaven cheeks reddened over the word. "Petticoats with 'Yankees, Go Home!' scrawled all over them! As innocent as a lurking Apache is what you are."

The sheriff paused to summon up suitable authority in his voice. "Will you come peaceably, or will the posse and me need to use force?"

"Just a moment, sir."

Lily was surprised to hear her oldest sister's voice. March pushed Tom's protective arm away, then spoke firmly.

"There's no point in involving our mama and daddy in this, sheriff. Neither Tom nor Rick. They *are* innocent. All of them. It's just that my sisters and I were upset over Daddy's hard times with the ranch. We planned and did the deed entirely by ourselves. To help Daddy save the ranch. And to strike a blow against the Damn Yankees!"

Her head went up when she said this, and Lily had never seen her big sister look so strong or beautiful before. She positively glowed through the twilight, her bunched-up hair almost like a halo around her heart-shaped face. Tom's eyes lit up in admiration, and his arm slipped back around her waist.

Not to be outdone, April continued the tale, her own charms taking on definition almost as strong as March's. "We just said

85

we were going to Enchanted Rock. We never made it farther than the butte by the trail. We hid up in that cave behind the back of it all afternoon, then walked back to the hills through the creek, so our footprints couldn't be followed."

Lily completed the confession. "And don't let Ned Brewster tell anybody he was almost shot within an inch of his life. I aimed for his jug and hit it square. There's no way we would have harmed a soul. Not even those Yankee officers sitting back in the coach. Mama trained us to be upright, and we Harper girls have our honor."

The sheriff's jaw had sunk, and his mouth was now open so wide a dozen horseflies could've swarmed inside before he remembered to close it. He finally barked out an order, and his posse headed for the girls. Daddy put up a hand and they stopped.

"Now, just a minute, here. Just one goldurned minute. I ain't letting you take my girls off like that. Nowhere and nohow. If they done what they said, for the reason they said, then I figure it must be my fault, although I had thought I'd instilled a finer set of morals in them . . . However that might be, I'm the one you want, not them."

The posse was rooted, waiting for the sheriff's response.

"Sorry, Harper. The Law don't work thataways. Though it might make life a heap easier on all of us." He nodded toward his men. "Take 'em away."

The six perpetrators were packed onto the posse's spare horses and led into the coming night. The sheriff was still shaking his head as he started off the parade, the Harper girls riding straight and proud to their destiny.

The last thing Lily heard was her mama's voice, breaking through her sobs. "But, Hy, I don't understand. I just don't understand any of this. And what about their clothing? They'll need clean dresses . . ."

It was a pitiful lament, and pure Mama through and through.

15

The posse rode through half the night under the pristine, starry Texas sky. When they got to Fredericksburg, it was still too dark to see much of the town. Anyway, the tiny adobe jailhouse sat on its edge. The sheriff had to roust two drunkards to clear space for the Harper girls. Groggy and grumbling, the men went home early to their wives.

There were only two beds, and those not more than straw-filled burlap mats. April touched one tentatively with her booted toe and claimed she saw lice hopping from it. After that, everyone picked a separate stretch of the hard-packed dirt floor and attempted to sleep.

The sun was high when Lily opened her eyes. But it wasn't that which woke her, because not much sun filtered in through the three tiny, barred windows of the jail. It was the noise. She eased herself up from the floor, brushed down her pants, and arched her back to get the creaks out of it. Jails didn't seem to be big on amenities. Standing on her tiptoes, she peeked out the nearest window, which opened onto the main street going through Fredericksburg.

It appeared they were fixing to have some kind of a fiesta out there. A crowd of people were milling around, more people than Lily had ever seen in her entire life. Men, women, children—children hanging on their mothers' skirts, or racing through the crowd with sticks and hoops, laughing like it was a holiday. Lily rubbed her eyes to remove some of the sleep and travel grit and looked again. Then June was next to her, shoving for a spot. There was a quick intake of breath.

"I declare, Lily," she whispered. "I do think they've come on account of us! Do you suppose we'll be famous?"

She quickly patted down the disarray of her frizzy hair, then waved enthusiastically. The crowd finally noted the movement and gave a cheer of approval. "I told you so!"

Lily grunted in disgust and left the window.

When O. T. Williams opened the heavy barred door that led into his adjoining office and started barking directions to a young man behind him, Lily figured they might be in jail for a while.

"Don't stand there gaping, Barly. Ain't you never seen law-breakers before? Get those filthy mats moved out!" He turned apologetically to the girls. "This here is Barly Bedlow, my deputy. He weren't in the posse last night on account of he was busy holding the fort right here in town."

All the girls were awake now, some of them still trying to tidy their hair without benefit of comb or brush. These min-istrations came to a halt as they stared up at Barly, a good two feet taller than his boss, with a head covered wildly in a mass of black curls. He was absolutely bullish in proportions. His smile, though, was gentle as he bestowed it first on all of them, then narrowed the favor down to May, who returned it with enthusiasm.

"My pleasure, ladies. I mean—"

"You mean nothing. Get to work!" shouted his boss.

The mats gone, a series of bedsteads, some more rickety than others, were pushed and prodded into the small room. The beds were followed by clean mattresses and bedding, and a pink porcelain pitcher and washbasin with painted medal-lions of buxom young ladies at their toilette. The sheriff di-rected the disposition of these items, then stood facing the girls for a moment, obviously ill at ease.

"The missus sent her favorite pitcher and bowl. She wants to know is there anything else you might need?"

April gave him her best smile. "That's right neighborly of her. Please thank her for us and ask maybe if she could spare a comb and a scrap of soap until our daddy and mama get some things to us?"

O.T. almost blushed. He seemed strangely prone to embarrassment for a man in his position.

"Ain't got no daughters myself, and never had no ladies as guests before, so if there's anything else of a, uh, more personal nature you might need . . ."

"Thank you kindly, Sheriff." It was March. "Maybe if we had a pencil and some paper, so we could write things down for your wife's eyes . . ."

"Surely, surely." He turned to go, then stopped at the door. "Oh, ah. The townfolks fixed up a little dinner for you, it being long gone for breakfast. All right if a few of 'em brings it in?"

"Are they going to see us like this?" June was suddenly conscious of the travel dust on her dress.

"What's the matter, June, stage fright all of a sudden? The show must go on."

"Lily, sometimes you can be so *mean*."

The sheriff made a quick escape. "I'll just send 'em in and out real fast like."

The food came in a steady stream for the rest of the day, passing through the plate-width grating set in the center of the bars on their door. There were tamales and chili and spicy stews from the Mexican population, potatoes and sausages and even wienerschnitzel from the Germans. Everyone wanted an excuse to inspect the Harper girls, and food seemed to be it.

The sheriff was still keeping his vigil propped up on a chair by the front door of the jail, where it was cooler, gun belt attached and rifle at his elbow. It was easy to keep an eye on him either from the front jail windows or their cell door, and Lily noticed that as the day wore on, he acted more and more like maybe it was a mistake to break this case like he had. There didn't seem to be anybody in the entire town getting anything done, O. T. Williams included. The brief glimpses the locals had had of the girls just seemed to excite more interest, from what Lily could tell. Even Barly acted a little demented every time he glanced in and caught sight of May's honey-colored head. Probably the only establishments doing business in Fredericksburg were the saloons.

It got so that by sundown, when Daddy and Mama appeared in the old buggy with fresh clothes and a pot of beans, their reception was not as enthusiastic as it might have been. The crowd, however, made way with some politeness when it was explained who it was coming into town. In front of the jail, Hy Harper jumped off, then raised his arms to help his wife down.

"Evenin', Sheriff."

"Evenin', Harper."

"Brung some things for my girls."

"Expected as much. I suppose you'll want to visit them, too."

"If that's all right."

"Don't know why not. Everybody else has."

The sheriff got up and fingered out the big key slowly from the ring around his belt.

"If I'd knowed there was gonna be so much ruckus, I might of dropped the whole thing."

"Wish'd you would have."

"Figured as much."

Hy Harper gestured toward the buggy. "I found something this morning maybe belongs to you. Hidden out in our stable."

The sheriff's eyebrows raised. "Yankee currency?"

"Appears to be the case."

"That'll be a help. It might ease things up some for your girls."

"Thought it might."

The door was finally swung open, and Mama, waiting silently

behind Daddy the whole time, finally burst past him into the jail cell, arms outstretched.

"My babies! Have they done anything terrible to you? Are you all right?"

"We're fit as a fiddle, Mama," answered Lily. "Except maybe for a little indigestion."

And then Mama was hugging and crying over every last one of them. She finally stopped when Daddy pulled her off.

"Enough, Gwen. You're acting like they was innocent or something."

"Of course they're innocent, Hy. How could my girls ever do what they said? They're *good* girls."

Lily felt a tiny pang of sorrow pierce her heart. Were all mothers like this? Would she be the same if she ever produced offspring? It must be mighty hard to do your best as you saw it, then have something like this crash on your head. It could make a person feel downright useless. She thought of all the schemes they'd tried before the holdup and hoped her mama never got wind of any of them. This here cross was enough for her to bear.

"You're right, Mama," Lily said. "We are good girls. Robbing a stagecoach just once to help out Daddy don't change any of that. Least, I don't see how it does. Our intentions were pure and honorable. And I might just do it again if I knowed for sure there was good, negotiable gold aboard."

"Hush yourself," March snapped. "That's not helping anything!"

"Sorry, March, but it's my true feelings."

"Then keep them to yourself. The rest of us have no intentions of pursuing a life of crime any further."

She looked at Daddy hovering behind by the door. "You didn't hear anything from Tom, did you?"

"Or Rick?" April added.

"Not since they left the Double H last night. And I hope to never see such a pair of bewildered young men again."

91

"They didn't say anything to you?"

"Just sort of mounted their horses and slunk off." Noticing his daughters' faces, he tried to improve the situation. "I wouldn't be too downhearted, though. A thing like this takes a little getting used to, is all." He glanced around. "Well, leastways they got you comfortable in here."

"For how long, Daddy?"

He regarded May. "I'm not sure. I have to track down a lawyer next. And find out when the circuit judge is due through." He prodded his wife. "Come along, Gwen. Let's get them their things. You can visit again in the morning before we head back home."

It was Lily who made the discovery, while the others were still snuffling after Mama and Daddy had gone. She'd been rifling through the pile of dresses and petticoats, only to find that Mama hadn't packed any clean shirts or britches for her. She actually expected Lily to dress up like a girl through this tribulation! Then her fingers hit upon something hard in the midst of lace and frills. She felt the object slowly. The significance of the long, rough-edged thing came to her in good time, whereupon she turned to the jail door, to make sure it was properly locked. It was, but she picked up a blanket and tucked it over the bars just the same. Barly was dozing by the rolltop desk beyond and opened one eye.

Lily smiled sweetly around the edge of the blanket. "I'm just arranging a little proper privacy for us, Barly. Night, now!"

He nodded and leaned back in the chair again.

Lily checked the high windows next. There were no prying faces there, either, just the darkness of the night that had settled in. A grin crept across her face. Julie looked over from her bed, then turned up the lamp the sheriff had thoughtfully left for them.

"What are you so all fired pleased about, Lily? Seeing Mama sorrowing like that, you can still smile?"

The others stopped dabbing at their tears and seemed ready to pounce on Lily, too, until she unveiled the hidden item.

"What is that?"

"Shh. Daddy's still watching over us, the best he can." She passed it around.

"A file? Does he expect us to keep shoeing the horses while we're here?"

"A file's got other uses, too, April." Lily nodded significantly toward the barred windows.

"You suppose we could actually get out of one of those?"

"We could, May, without all the petticoats and things."

"Why, it would take forever to saw through those bars!"

"Nobody's said anything about a trial date yet, June."

March was thinking. "It would have to be done in the dark. How would we disguise the progress?"

"I suspect Daddy thought of that as well." Sure enough, Lily retrieved a second object: a small pot of bootblack. "See?" She passed it around for inspection. "A dab of that rubbed on the bars when we're finished and you'd never know—"

Just then there was a discreet knock on the door. The incriminating file and bootblack were hidden under skirts, the blanket raised.

"Yes?"

The sheriff peeked through the bars. "It's been a long day, and we're both heading home to our beds. Anything else you'll be needing?"

"No, sir."

"Thank you just the same, sir."

"Will it be all right if we keep the lamp burning awhile, sir? To do some stitching?"

"And maybe throw a piece of cloth over the front windows, for more privacy?"

He reflected a moment. "You girls ain't planning on getting into any mischief, are you?"

"Honor bright."

"What kind of mischief you figure we could get into locked up in here?"

O.T. gave them a hard look. "I'm not at all sure. Still . . . Well, be good now."

And the outside door clanked shut.

They watched him through the window as he tucked his gun under his arm and walked off toward town, Barly's huge form trailing him sleepily. Thank goodness the rest of the people had left, too.

"All clear," whispered Lily.

June went first, and Lily sat back on her mattress to supervise. "Push that bed closer to the back window. Now start real low, June. That's it. Don't everybody push up so close. Give her some elbow room. There's four whole bars, and you'll all get a chance."

Lily considered while the others worked up a sweat. Even if it didn't work, it was nice to have something to do. If they could escape, where would they take off to? Mexico? The territories farther west? And what could they possibly do in any of those places?

The soft, steady grinding sounds lulled her until her head was on her chin and she was sound asleep.

16

☞ It wasn't but a few days before the reporters started showing up. First it was a man from the *San Antonio Express*, then someone from Houston, and finally several competing journalists from New York City. It was the Eastern journalists who created the most interest among the Harper girls.

"Just think of it. They heard about our little holdup clear out to the Atlantic Ocean," March said.

"We really are going to be famous!" whooped June.

"Fat lot of good that'll do any of us, June, if we end up swinging high," Lily shot back.

Her sisters stopped. They'd just been waltzing around the ramifications of their capture.

May gulped. "Surely they wouldn't do such a thing!"

"Nobody got hurt!" added April.

"Depends on the judge, whether he's a hanging one or not," Lily broke in. "You heard the sheriff discussing it with some of the local folks out front this morning. Then again, maybe you didn't. You were all fussing with each other's hairstyles. Anyhow, O.T. said something about whether the judge'd choose to make an example of us or not."

"Oh."

Lily sighed. "Stop weeping all over your embroidery, Julie. It won't help the sentiment." Julie was back to the **NO LEGACY** piece again. Mama had thoughtfully delivered it with their dresses. It was amazing how much progress Julie'd made on it with nothing else to distract her. She'd finished **HONESTY** all in bright red, and was presently working tiny bunches of yellow flowers with green stems and leaves in all the corners.

March was pacing now, between the beds. She finally raised her eyes from their focus on the dirt floor. "If that is so, then we'll have to do our best for Daddy and Mama while we can."

"I don't see how we can help them now," Lily protested.

"You wouldn't. You've never had bigger plans, like I've had."

Lily let it pass. "What did you have in mind?"

"We haven't really talked to any of those reporters yet. What if we agreed to do it only for money?"

All heads were at attention.

"They'd pay for something like that?" May asked.

"They would. To get the *true* story. And we wouldn't give it to but one paper."

March's words suddenly clicked with Lily. "You mean we'd make 'em bid on it, like at a cattle auction?"

"Precisely, little sister. Precisely. Highest bidder takes all."

It was the reporter from the *New York Herald* who won the auction, after a frenzied series of telegrams between Fredericksburg, Texas, and his home office. The girls had started their asking price high, at a thousand dollars. They figured that would cover all of Daddy's debts, plus some of the lawyer's fees that were sure to be coming home to roost soon. The other reporters had treated the Harper girls like maybe they were really crazy, all except for George Dunlop, the skinny, somber, gnome-like man who had covered most of the Civil War for the *Herald* and could smell a hot story from several thousand miles. This was just the trick needed to set his paper's circulation soaring back in New York during the dog days of August and into the fall. It would be a series, running right through the trial and its results, but beginning with the background of these lovely young ladies. He settled at five hundred dollars. It was an awe-inspiring amount for the Harper girls, even if it wouldn't take care of the bank loan completely.

George Dunlop had barely arrived at the jailhouse with a telegraphed credit chit as proof of payment, pencil and tablet at the ready, when he was shoved aside by a hot and dusty delegation from Izzy Henry's ranch. It was Tom and Rick come at last, followed, to everyone's surprise, by Ooh-long.

March and April's young men appeared embarrassed. Tom's hat was off, and his thick black hair clung wetly to his forehead. "It's not that we forgot about you, March. Or didn't plan to stand by you—"

"It's just what 'Pop' and 'Mother' would say, isn't that so, Tom?"

"Not at all!" His face burned red. "There's been a lot of branding to do, getting ready for the cattle drive, and this was the first Mr. Henry could spare us." He looked at Rick beseechingly.

Ooh-long ignored the unfolding drama and marched past the two young men, fixing his attention on Lily. He made a formal bow, then his excitement got the best of him. "I have letter!" He waved a crumpled sheet of Chinese calligraphy at Lily. "My bride comes by next ship from Hawaii! First daughter we have I name after you, Miss Lily!"

"May you be blessed with many sons before that, Ooh-long. My insignificance is not worthy of such an honor." Lily knew that kind of flowery language pleased her friend. "What's she like, Ooh-long? Is she pretty?"

"Didn't send picture. But young. Seventh daughter of big family. I think they happy to get rid of her. They no argue about price." Then he took in her surroundings. "You all right? Too small space in here. Lily needs big space."

"You're right there, friend." Lily had been getting cramped. They'd been let out once a day to exercise behind the jailhouse, under O.T.'s sharp surveillance, but it hadn't been enough. She'd been starting to miss Checkers, the comforting feel of his body underneath her as they wandered around the spread. "I'd just about give anything for a good gallop."

"Can't give gallop, but can give something else." Ooh-long reached behind him to deliver something into her hands.

"What is it? It smells good."

"Peking duck. Big treat for emperors of China. Also robber chieftains. They big people in China, too. Like you, now." He bowed again, in deference to Lily's new prominence. "Mister Henry, he not miss one duck, and apricots on tree just now ready for duck sauce." He frowned as Lily pulled off the newspaper wrapping and bit into one of the dainty pancakes stuffed with meat and scallions.

"Good?"

"Heavenly!" Lily swallowed another morsel with relish and focused back on the others. Apparently all had been forgiven, for Tom and Rick were taking distinct liberties with her big sisters.

"Hey! It ain't even nighttime yet!" she yelled.

March and April broke away from their embraces resentfully, and May gazed past them to Barly, in the office beyond, who was scratching his head at the scene. George Dunlop, the reporter, was madly dashing things down on his tablet, trying to get names from the Henry hands. "You there, sir, with the muttonchops. Are you affianced to Miss April?"

Rick glared at the wizened man with annoyance. "What's it to you? And ain't you a Yankee?"

Things kind of went downhill from there for a while.

May had been loath to ask Daddy to bring her his guitar, figuring that he might need it worse himself for consolation. She'd been discussing the subject with Barly, though, and that night, long after Tom and Rick had left, Barly showed up with a guitar for May. He slowly found the right key on his chain and pushed the instrument through the opening of the door, lowering his head to watch her response.

"It ain't handsome, Miss May, but it was the best I could find on short notice."

"Oh, Barly," she whispered as she fondled the scratched and battered instrument. "I hope you didn't go and spend all your pay on it!"

"Well, no. Fact is, I took it off a drunken cowpoke over to the Hi-Times Saloon just an hour back. He was busting things up some, and I told him it was a fine in lieu of incarceration."

May stared into his eyes. "I guess you'll be doing quite a bit of fining now that we're filling up your jail space."

"We got to do something to impress lawfulness on 'em all. Fact of the matter is"—he pulled a watch and fob from his pocket—"this here was another fine. It ain't nothing but a three-dollar timepiece, but I always did want one of my own." The normal-sized watch was dwarfed in his vast paw. "It ain't like I'm taking undue advantage, you understand. I wouldn't fine somebody a really good watch, or a family keepsake, like."

"I do understand what you're saying, Barly."

May had already tightened the guitar strings and was now testing the tone. Lily winced at the first chord. Funny thing about morality around here. It was all right for the sheriff's deputy to relieve drunks of their possessions, but it wasn't all right to perform a nice, clean robbery of a stagecoach that wouldn't hurt nobody but the insurance company. It sure was peculiar how the Law took to thinking.

May had finally gotten the guitar tuned and launched into a sprightly melody. Barly's foot, poking through the opening of the cell door, was tapping time. His feet were so big it would take most of a tanned hide just to outfit him in a pair of boots.

"My, but you have a way with that instrument, Miss May."

May made a silly moue with pursed lips. "Just find a piano for me, Deputy Barly, and see what I could do."

"You really hankering after a piano?"

"I am." Her fingers kept working, his toes tapping.

Barly ran a hand through his curls. "Well, might be a chance . . ."

The music stopped. "Really? How!"

"Not something I could fine away, though. Person in question is a mite too smart for that. It's Miss Bessie Blue, she's the town's chief madam—" He blushed when the realization of what he was mentioning to these young ladies hit him.

"What's a madam?" Julie wanted to know. She'd been following the conversation with the others, from want of anything better to do. Now the needle stopped its incessant plowing through her handiwork as she waited for an answer.

"It's a . . ." Barly reddened right up his cheekbones and down to his neck. "It's a lady what keeps a house where bachelors can go for a little company after working hours."

"What a fine, Christian idea," Julie commented. "There do seem to be so many more men than women around here. And they must get lonely sometimes." Her needle began its regular movements again.

Barly was dumbstruck for a long moment. "Anyhow, Miss Blue's been talking about moving on, farther west. Says it's been getting too civilized around here, now that we've got two churches and a school and everything. Her, uh, Christian work might be more needed elsewhere. And she's got a big old piano that she can't be carting off with her."

May was strumming again, faster. "I've got a little money coming to me, Barly. Would you mind asking what she'd accept for the piano?"

Lily saw her other sisters prick up, but they didn't say anything, not with Barly there.

"Sure thing, Miss May. Soon as I get a chance. Maybe even tonight. I'm locking up now, anyway."

And he did, very methodically. Lily watched him finally wander off down the road before she turned to May.

"Well, I guess you can just put down that guitar a minute,

May, and tell all of us what you mean by having a *little money* coming to you."

May looked at Lily, then at March and April, whose faces were more menacing.

"Well, I figured that a sixth of the newspaper money is rightfully mine, after all. That would be somewhere around eighty dollars."

"Eighty-three dollars and thirty-three cents," commented June.

"May, you know that money is for Daddy and his debts," Lily chided.

"Oh, pooh. I'm so tired of hearing about Daddy's debts. The whole amount isn't enough to satisfy all of them. And he'll probably just squander it on something else before it ever gets to the bank in San Antonio, anyway."

"Nevertheless," interrupted March. "Nevertheless, you are not to be thinking of spending it in that manner. Or any manner. Why, it could start off something. I could spend mine on that sewing machine for Mama, and lots of pretty cloth—"

"And it would be near enough a stake to let me and Rick get married," continued April.

"And think of all the buckets of paint—dozens of colors—I could buy for Mama and the house with my share," Lily added, just to make the point. "And I'm sure June and Julie could think of something, too."

"You bet, why—"

The oldest took them in hand. "Enough! We won't discuss any of this again. Ever."

They didn't, for a while. They were too busy telling their story to George Dunlop the next day. And getting ready for the circuit judge, who was due in town momentarily.

17

☞ It was another hot morning when the Harper girls were marched off to the courtroom behind the lobby of the Fredericksburg Hotel. It wasn't always a courtroom. Barly mentioned it was mainly used for dances, except when the judge was in attendance. Anyway, the hotel was the biggest building in town, made out of the pale brown local stone, and had a good solid quality to it.

Lily's sudden interest in all of these otherwise irrelevant details was born of a single emotion: fear. She was scared silly. More scared than when she'd lain awake most of the night before the robbery. So scared she needed to think of *anything* else.

For example, the outfit she was wearing, which also tended to put her out of sorts. It was hot. Lily scratched behind her neck, where the high collar itched, then under her arm, where the dress was too tight. She just happened to be built a whole lot broader than her sisters, sort of the difference between a slim foal and a newborn calf. March and April had had to jam her into it. It was a dark blue wool poplin, trimmed in red flannel. It was out of season and way above her ankles, but she guessed it was altogether the best Mama could come up with on short notice. It wasn't like Mama'd had that much practice with Lily, after all.

Barly was also to blame for how she was feeling at this

moment, as she walked down Main Street like a trussed turkey. It was he who'd taken to regaling the girls with Judge Wiley stories.

Barly'd begun in the long hot night after they'd finished telling their own story to George Dunlop. Maybe hanging around listening had put him in that frame of mind. Anyway, they'd all been anxious to curtain the windows and door and strip down to their chemises or less on account of the pervading heat, but couldn't because Barly had no mind to walk himself home. He'd just sat there, tipped back in the desk chair that creaked on iron springs, with his gigantic feet propped up against the bars of their cell door. Then he started in. "O.T. says as how Judge Wiley is expected in town in another day or two."

The girls didn't take the bait, too enervated even to fan themselves with the brand-new paper fans the local undertaker had been kind enough to drop by that morning. The fans lay in a pile at the foot of one bed, **GUMBERT'S OF FREDERICKSBURG. CARPENTRY, COFFINS, UNDERTAKING. NO JOB TOO LARGE OR TOO SMALL!** emblazoned all over them in bold black print.

"It puts me in mind of the time the judge sat sentencing on the Smith brothers," Barly added, trying again. "They was horse thieves."

May finally bit. "What are they now, Barly?"

"Six feet under. In the cemetery t'other side of town. Gumbert, the old vulture, came to visit them in jail, too, and cozened them out of their lucky twenty-dollar gold pieces the day of their trial. Promised 'em genuine mahogany hardwood coffins, he did. But they got buried in soft pine like anybody else. Gumbert, he went grinnin' straight to the bank after the funeral."

Lily was certain the cell's temperature had dropped noticeably. Julie's hand was up to her throat, and March and April appeared downright chilled.

Barly didn't seem to take any notice. He pulled a cheroot

out of his shirt pocket and lit it up with a match struck on his boot sole. "Then there was what Judge Wiley done with a guilty verdict to the Tilghman gang down to Bandera."

Lily was caught now. "What had *they* done?"

"A touch of light bank robbery. Only it got serious when they lost their tempers and shot down a customer or two unexpected like." He waved his hand in the air, the cheroot like a toothpick lost in it. "The Bandera folks worked up their civic pride and built a row of four execution stands, right in the middle of their plaza, so the whole gang could be lynched at the same time. O.T. was down to watch and says it was just like a fiesta."

"Well." Lily could hear June let out her pent-up breath clear across the cell. "Well. We certainly never hurt anybody!"

"Wiley, he don't think much of cattle rustlers, neither."

There was a new hush as the girls delved into their minds back to the Izzy Henry business.

"Take that time last summer when Otis Lee and Billy Joe Hudspeth were brought in from clear over in Blanco County. They said as how they were only using a little free enterprise. The judge, he said enterprise never been that free, even in Texas."

"Did he hang them, too?" Julie was closer to tears than usual.

"Nope. Must've been one of Wiley's soft days. Just give 'em twenty years in the state penitentiary to rethink their views on economics. They'll be out in only another nineteen."

Barly inspected his half-smoked cheroot and eased out of the sheriff's chair. He stretched himself clear up to the ceiling.

"Guess I'll be heading home. You ladies sleep well, now." He stopped to give May a special smile, which for once she didn't return, then blew out the lamp on the desk and lumbered out the door.

The Harper girls stared at each other until they could no longer hear his footsteps. Julie started the flood by wiping a slow tear from the corner of an eye with her needlework.

"I want to go home to Daddy and Mama!"

"Now, Julie . . ." tried March. But it was no good. She delved into a pocket for the notorious handkerchief and blew her own nose lustily. "I guess maybe I want to go home, too."

"Just think what Judge Wiley did to all those people." It was June, saying what was only too obvious. "What's he going to do to us?" Her eyes lit on Gumbert's gift of fans, and she attacked one, viciously tearing it to shreds. "To think of that, that *undertaker* sniffing around us today, like maybe we were potential business!"

"Maybe we are," Lily said. "Maybe we should stop playing games with ourselves. I know we tried to do our best by Daddy, but maybe we ought to have rethought things right at the beginning of the summer, when this all begun."

"You mean stood up to him? Disobeyed him?" May was incredulous.

"Could be. Comes a time a person's got to make up her own mind about what's right and what's wrong. What we done was wrong."

"That's easy for you to say now, Lily," commented March from the depths of Mama's square of Irish linen. "Why didn't you say something three months ago?"

It was Julie who spoke up. "I said something, but nobody paid any attention! I fought the target practice and everything!"

"I hadn't worked it out back then, not like Julie," Lily continued. "Not all the way through, although I did suggest the Longhorns. I guess I was just looking at helping Daddy solve his problem the quickest way. And maybe I was looking at the fun side, too. Besides, the good Lord blessed the lot of us with consciences, not only Julie. Don't go chiding me for having picked what seemed like the easiest road."

"Ah, yes," murmured June. "The Road to Ruin. How smooth it seemed. How quickly it led us from the path of virtue."

There was a pained pause during which Lily got up to fix the window curtains and blow out the lamp. Darkness surrounded them, but not silence. There were going to be a lot of damp pillowcases in the morning.

So there was Lily, the day of the trial, walking kind of pigeon-toed down Main Street, because she didn't noways know how to handle her petticoats and skirts, muttering imprecations to Barly under her breath for again having awakened in the lot of them something they'd have rather left dormant. Her five sisters were in their summer best, marching like queens to the scaffold in front of her. Guilt hadn't changed them so much that they hadn't gotten up before dawn to show themselves to their best advantage on this critical day. But as for Lily, she vowed then and there if she ever got out of this mess alive, they'd have to tie her up to get her into another dress anytime soon.

The townfolks had gotten bored with feeding the girls a long time past, but they'd still managed enough interest to line the boardwalks on either side of the street. The open range never called to Lily as strong as it did that day. All she wanted to do was jump on the nearest horse and hightail it out of there. Unfortunately, Barly was leading the procession, and the sheriff himself, not being anybody's fool, was keeping a tight hold of the rear, shotgun at the ready. Lily knew then what cattle must feel like on a roundup. Doomed.

That first morning went kind of slow: merely the jury being chosen, and the case stated. It gave Lily the time to study Judge Wiley carefully, on account of he held the reins to their future, if there was any. Course, the jury might have a say in that, too, but after hearing all those stories of Barly's, Lily had the feeling this judge might be more important than the whole jury put together. If they were called in guilty.

Judge Wiley was an older man, maybe fifty or more. He was bald on top—not as much as Daddy, though. Or maybe it just appeared that way because he didn't try to disguise his affliction any. Neither did he seem to pay it any attention. It was merely a fact of life. There was this round, pale expanse, surrounded by coarse salt-and-pepper hair that grew right around his ears into a full salt-and-pepper beard. He was medium height, with a comfortable build, which gave him the aspect of being well fed and nicely looked after his entire life. His eyes were a deep blue, and while he didn't let on to having an ounce of humor in his body, Lily noticed a curious twinkle in them now and again.

And then there was how Judge Wiley dressed. No leather vests and boiled shirts for him. He wore a dove-gray summer ditto suit that looked to be some kind of silk. March would no doubt have loved a matching dress out of the stuff. The frock coat had a long skirt to it, and had his tight-fitting waistcoat been in bright paisley, you could have took him for a gambling man. Then there was his crisp white shirt, meticulously arranged tie, and straw hat for the summer heat, not to mention his thin, elegant cane. To say he seemed out of place in Gillespie County was an understatement.

Of course, the same could be said of Aaron Jones, to whom Lily turned her attention after she'd finished trying to figure out the judge. Daddy'd tried his level best with the lawyer, like everything else, only the one he'd ended up with was no prize. But then, there weren't that many lawyers to be had in Gillespie County, either.

Mr. Jones was short and potbellied, and did not seem overbright. Maybe it was that stringy blond hair combed back from his forehead in greasy clumps that was so off-putting. Or the way he never went anywhere without his whiskey flask. Including *court*! He'd cough self-consciously, make as though he was missing a few papers, and duck under the table for a quick nip. He thought nobody was watching, but in fact everyone in the place would pause, fascinated, from the judge and jury on down, till he'd surface with a self-congratulatory smirk. It made Lily right glad the Harper still had exploded like it had. She couldn't stand the thought that Aaron Jones might be drinking Harper moonshine otherwise.

Thinking back, though, he did seem to be trying to help out with the case. Maybe his looks and behavior were deceiving.

From the outset, during his first brief visit to the jail cell, he'd insisted the Harpers plead not guilty. Lily had thought about his words for a while, then bust out: "But the sheriff already *knows* right enough we done it."

"It don't matter, little girl."

"Beg your pardon, but I'm *not* a little girl!"

"Well, excuse me. I'm not accustomed to dealing with juvenile offenders." He took a healthy swig from his flask before continuing. "It's like this. In the Law of these United States, it don't matter a fig whether a person is truly guilty or truly innocent. It's what the jury believes." He swiped at his lips with his coat sleeve, adding another stain to his already soiled, preacher-black coat. "So you see, there's no point whatsoever in predisposing that jury unfavorably."

After the Harpers had all cogitated awhile, his words seemed to make a certain amount of sense, so the girls agreed to go along with him.

"And one more thing, young ladies."

"Yes, Mr. Jones?"

"This business about the signs, or slogans, or whatever you want to call what you were wearing?"

They were all looking on him with interest now.

"It occurs to me we might just emphasize that angle. From a patriotic point of view, of course. You get my meaning?"

Maybe, just maybe, Aaron Jones was not as hopeless as he let on.

Lily had almost fallen asleep when a break was declared and everybody went off to the hotel dining room for their dinners, the Harpers included.

Lily dug into her chicken-fried steak with gusto. It was the biggest piece of meat she'd seen in a long time, and the dull-ness of the morning's business had made her momentarily cast her guilty conscience and fear to the winds.

"The county paying for this, sheriff?"

"Unfortunately, yes."

At the thought, O.T. seemed to view his own hunk of meat less enthusiastically. Her sisters had all gone for the chicken, and Lily caught Barly, his mouth full, watching May delicately dismember her white meat. He sure was fascinated by her. Lily wondered if it was May's notoriety, or just May.

Barly swallowed. "I never did get back to you on that piano, Miss May."

"Yes?"

"Miss Blue, well, she says she couldn't part with it for less than seventy-five dollars, it being what she calls an upright grand and all. But my feeling is she'd go lower if she was asked nicely."

"How much less?"

He had another hunk of meat on his fork, and waved it around. "Ten, maybe fifteen dollars."

May shot a sly look at March, who was choking on her chicken. "That would allow a piece of my eighty-three-dollar newspaper share left over for Daddy, sister dear." Acting like that justified everything, May didn't bother waiting for March's protest, but turned her attention back to the deputy sheriff. "Thank you kindly, Barly. Would you mind proceeding with the negotiations for me?"

"Not at all. Not at all."

O.T. glanced up suspiciously. "What's this about a piano?"

"I'm thinking of acquiring one, Sheriff." May smiled sweetly.

He stared at May and the rest of them like they were all sheer demented. Talking pianos at a time like this, with life or death hanging overhead. Then he grunted.

"As long as you don't try dragging it into the jail. There ain't enough room to turn around in there anymore with all you girls and your things. Barly, you give 'em permission to store their extra dresses and bonnets in my office?"

Barly was still chewing, unconcerned. He was already on his second steak and could probably handle another two or three easily. "It seemed like a reasonable request, O.T. Women's things do take up a heap of space."

O.T. looked pained for a moment, then shoved back his barely touched plate. "Finish up. It's time to get back to court."

Lily was still mopping up the gravy on her plate. She gave the sheriff a disappointed frown.

"But I was so hoping for some of that apple pie!"

O.T. just grimaced back.

"No apple pie?"

"This ain't a Sunday social, no matter how you girls been working it. No apple pie."

Daddy and Mama turned up that afternoon in court. Mama was spruced up nicer than Lily could ever remember her, downright pretty in her sprigged muslin dress. Even Daddy had shaved and changed into a clean shirt. Some people made room for them right behind the defendants, so the family could catch up on the gossip in whispers.

"Who's taking care of the ranch, Daddy?" asked Lily.

"Rick is. At least for today and part of tomorrow. He got Izzy's permission to stay behind there and catch up with the cattle drive later, while we see to this court business. That's what took us so long, going over a few things with him."

"Isn't Rick an angel!" murmured April.

"He certainly is. Let's just hope you won't be one soon."

"Daddy!" March was shocked.

"Hush up, girl. Judge Wiley is trying to get on with business."

"Just a minute." Lily put her head closer and lowered her voice even more. "Where are you staying tonight?"

It was Mama who answered. "Well, you know, dear, we haven't a penny left. Not since your daddy spent that gold piece

110

he found on the lawyer and our lodgings the last time . . . We thought maybe that nice sheriff would let us bunk down in jail with you girls. You've got everything set up so comfortably there—"

"Ssh!"

"Order in the court!"

Where in tarnation would they all fit? Lily supposed the girls could triple up, leaving a bed for Mama and Daddy, but O.T. wasn't going to be real pleased. Anyway, it was time to get back to business.

Not much more happened in court that afternoon, except all of the Harper girls had to get up and answer a bunch of questions after swearing on the big Bible that sat in front of Judge Wiley, right next to his *Revised Statutes of Texas*. From March on down to Julie, the same story was recounted about the robbery. Then they got to Lily, who stood up and started into the identical story again, until Judge Wiley exploded.

"How in the name of heaven can you Harper girls be pleading not guilty to this robbery? You each and every one of you admit to being at the scene of the crime, down to the smallest details!"

"Well, sir, it's like this," Lily said. "First off, our lawyer, Mr. Jones, he told us there was no point in predisposing the jury against us by admitting otherwise . . ." Lily gave the jury a nice smile at this point, and they all smiled back. A good lot they seemed to be, all solid townfolks. Some of them had even brought the Harpers food their first few days in jail.

"That's the correct term, ain't it, sir? 'Predisposing'?" That's when she saw the first hint of a glimmer in those eyes that had been all icy blue for hours. He nodded yes, so she just went on.

"And next, and more important, we really are innocent, on account of the lark was meant from the start as a message to those Yankees that we Texans ain't given up the struggle and hunkered down under their yoke quite yet." Lily waited for the cheer from the crowd to die down. It appeared Aaron Jones had been barking up the right tree after all with his final piece of advice.

"And the money had nothing to do with it?"

"Well, sir, to tell you true, it might have been a help to save our poor daddy's ranch. Him that's been scraping and struggling for years to make an honest go of it. Him that never had a dishonest bone in his body."

She was crossing her fingers behind her back at this point, but nobody noticed. "Anyway, a little gold would have been right nice. And we would have paid it all back when we got on our feet again. But it wasn't nothing in that box but Yankee currency, and you all know how worthless that is!"

There was a hum of agreement.

"Besides, that was all returned, so no one's the worse. Except maybe the U.S. Army, who couldn't catch a herd of innocent Texas girls right under their noses."

Lily had to stop there, because the courtroom was in an uproar of shouts and clapping. Judge Wiley himself had pulled out a fine linen handkerchief to hide his own smile, and Lily gave him a teeny wink. He finally put the handkerchief down and banged on the table with his gavel. The last snickers died off into hiccups of sheer pleasure. Even George Dunlop, all business in his role as the Harpers' official press biographer, had cracked a smile.

"So you still assert you are completely innocent?"

Lily's eyes opened as wide as they could. "Of course, Judge, sir. I just don't understand how a little lark, a bit of high spirits, could land us all in jail for this length of time. It must be costing the county plenty, and I could think of better ways to spend the county's money."

Judge Wiley swallowed back down something that seemed to be rising from his throat right up into his salt-and-pepper beard. "Thank you, Miss Lily. You may step down."

Lily did, then waited.

The judge looked at all six of the Harper girls, then at the rest of the courtroom.

"This court is dismissed until tomorrow morning. The jury will reconvene at nine sharp to deliberate on their verdict."

So they were all sent back to the jailhouse.

18

☞ O.T. wasn't any more delighted about keeping a hotel than Lily had expected, but he didn't really have much choice, short of taking Daddy and Mama home with him. They stayed.

After they'd been locked in for the night and their jailers had headed home, the girls tried to make Mama and Daddy as comfortable as possible. But Daddy was interested in one thing only. He peered out all the windows carefully before covering them over with the makeshift curtains. "What I want to know is what kind of progress you've been making with my tools."

Julie jumped up to show him the bars of the rear window. She'd taken a proprietary interest in the project at nights, to the detriment of her stitching. June had expended a lot of her pent-up energies on the iron, too, playing the whole time that she was the Count of Monte Cristo. The fact was, Lily hadn't gotten but a few licks in with the file the whole time, the others were so fascinated by it.

"Come see, Daddy," Julie said. "We've got three sawed through entirely, and the fourth just has a quarter of an inch left at the top!"

Daddy removed a bar and inspected it with enthusiasm before jamming it back into place. He turned around, beaming. "Excellent! I always knew you girls could fend for yourselves in a pinch. Let me have that file. We want to be good and ready if the jury doesn't come through tomorrow."

"Why wouldn't they, Daddy?" asked Julie.

"Can't say myself, but if they don't, I wouldn't trust that Wiley further than I could spit. They say he's the toughest judge on sentencing in the entire state of Texas." He ignored his daughters' too-knowing looks to smile at Mama, who had her worried frown on again. "Not to worry your pretty head, Gwen dear. The girls'll be let off. If not, they're ready to be let out." He pointed at the window with meaning, then got to work with a will.

There was much tossing and turning in bed that night. Lily hardly got a wink of sleep, stuffed in the middle between June and Julie like she was. She tried pinching them a couple of times to calm them down, but that didn't seem to work, either. Lily only prayed that if the lot of them were spared the rope and ended up in a real jail, a penitentiary, the keepers would have the sense to parcel them all out into separate rooms. There couldn't be much worse than spending twenty or so years cramped up with a slew of older sisters.

The jury only took an hour to deliberate the next morning. They returned grinning from the saloon of the hotel where they'd been sequestered, wiping beer suds from their whiskers. Lily assumed they'd finally had a chance to act on Aaron Jones's bibulous inspiration.

Judge Wiley scrutinized the lot, then asked if they'd reached a verdict.

"We have, your honor."

"And would you mind sharing it with the defendants and myself?"

The jury foreman smirked. "Not at all, your honor. We good citizens of Fredericksburg County . . ." He paused here to smooth back his hair and pull at his vest, thereby adding to the knots in Lily's stomach, before starting in again. "We good citizens of Fredericksburg County find the Harper girls totally and completely . . ." He paused again, and Lily thought she'd die for sure, before he finally blurted out: "Innocent!"

The courtroom had been jam-packed that morning, with the locals sitting and hanging on everything but the room's chandelier. Now they exploded into a good-humored cheer and stomping that set the floors to shaking. The banned Confederate flag was pulled from secreted places and waved in the air, along with a few Lone Star flags.

"Yahoo!"

"Up with Dixie!"

"Remember the Alamo!"

Lily almost expected a band to come parading in, adding to the din of the moment. For herself, she sighed with relief. They'd pulled it off. Guilty or not, Southern sentiment still prevailed in Texas. But she wouldn't care to try the system again. Ever.

Her sisters were hugging each other and anybody else at hand. The sheriff's wife was holding smelling salts under Mama's nose. Daddy was preparing to add to the general confusion by lighting up a huge cigar someone had shoved at him. Judge Wiley still sat, unmoving, at the table in the front of the room. On a hunch, Lily threaded through the crowd, up to him.

"Thank you kindly, Judge."

"For what, Miss Harper? It's the jury you should be thanking."

"Still and all . . . You really wouldn't have sent us to the penitentiary, would you?"

"My dear young lady, the penitentiary would have been

115

unworthy of your talents. I predict much greater things for you and your sisters!" And picking up his straw hat and cane, the good Judge Wiley disappeared into the still-raucous crowd.

Completely free, the Harpers made their first stop the Fredericksburg Bank, where they cashed their *New York Herald* check. It was written out, "Five hundred dollars payable to bearer in gold coin." They'd made sure enough of the gold part with George Dunlop after their other experience with Yankee currency. They were slow learners, but they were learning.

There was a slight altercation between members of the family on Main Street as to how it was to be spent. Lily contended that the entire amount should be sent directly to San Antonio to cover most of Daddy's debt. It was Daddy who protested. He was feeling high and happy, another vast cigar poking from his mouth. He only gagged on the smoke a few times.

"I thank you for the sentiment, Lily, but it would still be a full hundred dollars short of the requested amount. And a body ought to celebrate after what we all been through. In for a penny, in for a pound."

"But, Daddy—"

"Don't go Daddying me like that, daughter. We Harpers been down so long, it's time we looked up at the sky a little."

"Hy dear, perhaps Lily has a point about that loan . . ."

He turned to Mama and beamed at her through the smoke. "Don't fuss, Gwen. I know what I'm doing. Now then, girls, it seems to me a few of you have been hankering after some new duds . . ."

There were squeals of excitement from all save Lily. She tried to pull at her sisters' skirts, tried to throw some sense into their heads, but it was for naught. All that business about using their brains and consciences just plain evaporated before the temptation of a little brightly colored cloth. Fling in a few glass beads and a trade blanket and the Harpers would be in the same position as the Indians. And to think that just a few hours earlier they were worried about actually saving those same heads and necks. It didn't make a whole lot of sense.

After paying off the lawyer and sending a hundred dollars to the bank in San Antonio—a small concession to quiet Lily and let the powers that be know Daddy was still working on his foreclosure problem—they drove out of town in the wagon that afternoon with long-overdue staples for the larder, one upright grand piano (its price suitably negotiated by Barly), a sewing machine, bolts of dressmaking cloth with assorted paraphernalia, and a stack of the latest fashion magazines, only a few months old. June was clutching *The Autobiography of an Actress* by a Mrs. Anna Cora Mowatt that had been gathering dust in a corner of the Fredericksburg general store. Asked what she wanted, Lily refused anything until she realized her continued protest was hopeless. All that money was being squandered away right under her nose. She settled for several tubs of bright paint for the house.

 It was a Saturday afternoon not more than a week later. Lily was painting the ranch-house shutters a geranium red, one eye fixed on the sky. Somehow, with all the excitement, mid-September had snuck up on them. It appeared to be bringing with it the annual monsoons, too, from the look of some wicked clouds on the horizon. It was probably already storming down to the Henrys'. Not that hardly anybody was at the Henrys' to notice. Practically the whole lot—with the exception of Mrs. Henry, who'd gone off for her fall season in San Antonio—had long since lit out with the herds north to Kansas and the waiting railroad. Even Ooh-long. While the girls were still waiting their trial, Izzy had contracted to take along the few score of cattle Daddy had worthy of selling. There certainly weren't enough to justify Daddy's joining the drive.

So March and April had missed a reunion with their young men and wouldn't be seeing them for a while. That pill hadn't gone down too hard, since they had their new toys to play with. Her sisters had been running that new Singer sewing machine near to death for the past week—and with the pile of cloth they'd brought home, it might even be enough to keep them content through the winter. Between the machine with its steady whir, the sounds of May singing as she plunked on her piano, and June declaiming from choice bits of Mrs. Mowatt's book, one would think that everything was perfect around the Double H.

Well, it wasn't. Lily took another gander at the sky, then began putting away her brush and paint. What she should've asked for was roofing supplies. There was going to be a god-awful uproar when that rainstorm caught the roof holes and started drenching the new piano and sewing machine.

There hadn't been enough money left, anyhow. Who'd ever think that five hundred dollars could wither away so fast? In an afternoon? And here was Daddy still in debt up to his ears and over, and no place for fresh money to come from. He'd been puffed up like a little fighting cock that afternoon in Fredericksburg. All self-confidence and pride and on top of the world, with his daughters vindicated and spending money in his pocket. Maybe that's the way he'd been when he'd first courted Mama, before realities set in. But the last few days Lily had watched him slowly deflate. She just didn't know where he'd come up with any more cash-making plots and plans. It seemed like they'd used every one of them up.

Lily hauled her equipment back to the stable. Coming out, she gave the house an appraising glance. It was more cheerful already. And after she'd painted the window frames that fine powder blue— But what was the point? In a few more months it would all belong to the bank. The ranch house and the sticky-black plot of kitchen garden beyond, and the acres and acres of hills . . .

The rain and hoofbeats came almost simultaneously. Lily wasn't sure they weren't one and the same until she made it to the veranda and stood shaking herself like a half-drownded dog, squinting off across Hollering Woman Creek. The sky was storm-black, but she could still make out a huge figure galloping through the creek and up to the house. It wasn't till that figure had dismounted from an equally impressive horse and came stomping up the steps that she recognized him.

"Barly Bedlow! What in the name of goodness are you doing all the way out here?"

"Howdy, Miss Lily. Sorry I brung the weather with me. But we did need it." Then he just stood there, water dripping from his hat.

"You be wanting to see my sister May?"

He grinned. "Don't mind if I do, at that. Also, I got a message for you all."

Lily stuck her head in the door and bellowed out, "Company!" Just to give them notice. Then she turned back to the deputy sheriff. "How's O.T. holding up without us?"

"I do think he misses you. It's been mighty quiet and slow, ever since—"

Suddenly all the girls were at the door.

"Barly!"

"Come right in!"

"How could you leave him standing on the veranda, Lily!"

Lily shrugged and ran out into the rain to tend to his horse.

She guessed they'd have to put up Barly on the parlor rug tonight. Couldn't anybody expect a man to ride another thirty miles through this weather in the dark.

It took a while for Barly Bedlow to get to the purported reason for his visit. First he had to be dried down. That took just about every shred of toweling they had, along with the willing hands of Lily's sisters. They all treated him like he was their long-lost big brother, giggling and fussing over him like that. Except for May. She took to him more like March or April might have taken to their own beaus in similar circumstances, without any of the sneaky hugging, though. It hadn't quite come to that yet between them, and besides, Mama was standing right by the whole time, making sure it didn't.

Next Barly had to listen to May's progress on the piano, and admire the new frocks the Harper girls had been stitching together. Only after promising that he *would* stay to supper and he *would* spend the night did he remember to pull a flimsy telegraph message from his pocket.

"It come addressed to you all care of the Fredericksburg jail." He passed it to Daddy, who had just emerged from the weather himself.

The telegram was crushed and damp, but still legible. Daddy fingered it for a moment while Mama stood behind him, fidgeting. "It's nothing bad, I hope, Hy? Nobody dead?"

"Don't fret. We don't know nobody that could afford to send us a telegraph message if they kicked off, Gwen."

At last Daddy read out the missive:

**DELIGHTED HERALD ACCOUNTS TEXAS EXPLOITS STOP OF-
FER HARPER GIRLS ONE HUNDRED DOLLARS WEEKLY TOP
BILL PASTORS OPERA HOUSE FOR REENACTMENT SAME STOP
FOUR WEEKS GUARANTEED WITH POSSIBLE TOUR AFTER
STOP WIRE BACK COLLECT IF INTERESTED STOP DETAILS
FOLLOW STOP TONY PASTOR**

Daddy was puzzled. "Anybody hear tell of this Tony Pastor?"
Nobody had.

"It would be in New York City, I reckon. A hundred dollars a week." His eyes ate up the message again. Then he looked at Mama. The rest of them were too awestruck to make any comment.

"It could be the answer, Gwen. To everything."

Mama just gasped. "My daughters, on the *stage*? It isn't decent. Is it, Hy?"

June broke in. She quoted a verse from her new book, launching into it with enthusiasm:

> *Ne'er heed them, Cora, dear,*
> *The carping few who say*
> *Thou leavest woman's holier sphere*
> *For lights and vain display.*

"That was way back in 1845, Mama, after she wrote *Fashion*. Mrs. Mowatt showed the world that a decent woman *could* go on the stage. It couldn't ruin our reputations anymore, not in this modern day and age!"

Fine for June to be getting all worked up about this, thought Lily—she who'd been near dying for the chance to even see a play. But actually to get up and stand there in front of a crowd of paying people . . . It wouldn't be at all the same as in the courtroom, when the whole town was on their side, getting their entertainment free. And it wasn't reputations that bothered Lily, either. She didn't figure they had much left in that department anyhow, after that stagecoach-robbery business. There'd be dresses that would have to be worn, and the leaving of Texas . . . Then again, four hundred dollars guaranteed, and maybe more, could go a long way toward stopping the foreclosure.

"I ain't crazy about it, but I guess you can count me in. It'll only be for a month or two of the ranch's slow season. And maybe it'll save the place for Daddy."

Everybody stopped to digest Lily's rapid assessment of the situation. Then the others started casting in their lots.

It took Julie the longest to agree. She did it sniffling into her handkerchief. "If it will help Daddy and Mama like Lily says, I suppose I'll have to make the sacrifice, too. At least it's honest work."

Barly was bewildered. "You mean you all're just going to pick up and take off for the wickedness of New York City and something you don't know? Just like that?"

"Not just like that," March replied. "Get me something to write on, somebody. We have to compose an appropriate reply."

Maybe she was thinking that Tom Carter hadn't yet proposed, and wasn't likely to. Not with him due back East in another month or so after the cattle drive. Maybe she was figuring that a tour might take in Wilmington, Delaware. At any rate, she went about writing up that reply like she negotiated for the stage every day of her life.

" 'Dear Mr. Pastor.' No. That uses up too many words. He'll think us profligate from the start. 'Re Harper Girls engagement.' " She smiled brightly. "Does that sound businesslike enough, Daddy?"

Daddy was somehow short of words for once.

" 'Re Harper Girls engagement. Consider deal final if you guarantee round-trip transport, room and board while engaged, and $600 minimum (gold species). Availability on call, care of Double H Ranch, Gillespie County, Texas.' " March smiled with satisfaction. "That should take care of stagecoach and train fare all right!"

June broke in. "I think you ought to add one more thing, March. In Mrs. Mowatt's book it mentions that a lot of the stage people are responsible for their costumes out of their own salaries. That might get expensive, too."

"Excellent point, June. I dub you official bookkeeper in this little enterprise." She worked with the wording once more. "'Guarantee round-trip transport, costume expenses, room and board while engaged, and $600 minimum (gold species).' Does that suit everyone?"

"It suits me just fine," Lily said, "except there's one thing I mean to make clear here and now!"

"What could that be, Lily?"

Lily gave May a wicked eye. "You get a yearning for any more pianos, May, or you, April and March, for any more fancy duds, just remember this enterprise is in favor of saving the ranch for Daddy. We don't any of us get a cut until all his debts are paid, free and clear! Otherwise there'll be the devil to pay from me, Lily Harper!"

Mama gasped at Lily's profanity, and Julie pulled the handkerchief up to her mouth, presumably to mask her horror, but they all seemed to take her seriously enough.

"That's all I got to say. I think it's my turn to cook tonight, Mama. You have any special menu in mind, seeing as how we've got a guest?"

Barly still had his mouth open, muttering, "Just like that?"

It was nearly just like that. Barly played messenger with the exchange of telegrams, not seeming to mind either the long ride out from the county seat, or the time away from his boss, since May was waiting at the end of the journey, ready to cosset him and play a new song for him.

In ten days, the Harper girls were back in Fredericksburg, where they would meet the stagecoach. The Henry hands were still off on the cattle drive, so neither Rick nor Tom knew what their sweethearts were up to. It was just as well. There was no way they would have approved.

Daddy had driven his daughters into town in the wagon and now waited around with them for the coach. Mama had wanted to come, too. In fact, she'd wanted to make the entire trip with them as chaperone. But Daddy had pointed out that his girls were old enough and had enough sense by this time to look after their own better interests. Besides, Tony Pastor hadn't sent any extra travel money for chaperones.

Barly was waiting, too, giving May longing glances. He finally got up the nerve to say something as they heard the coach coming into town.

"Now see here, May." They'd gotten past the "Miss" part a few visits back.

"Yes, Barly?" She stood gazing up at him, dwarfed into an even more delicate package by his giantness.

"Well. Uh." His hand ruffled nervously through his mop of black curls, shoving them more askew than usual. "Well, you just take good care of yourself, hear? And when you get back . . ."

"Yes, Barly?"

It was sheer disgusting the way the two were mooning over each other. Lily could hardly stand it.

"Well, when you get back, maybe we can have a serious talk. I got my own little house, right here in town. And a steady salary—"

The coach to San Antonio pulled up, Ned Brewster himself holding the reins. He spotted the Harper girls and reached for his jug protectively. Lily stopped following the other conversation and grinned up at him.

"Don't worry, Ned. I left my rifle back at the ranch! Say, can I sit up front next to you? It looks a mite stuffy in the back."

Ned blanched, right up to his bulbous red nose. But he moved over.

After hugging their daddy goodbye, the Harper girls were on their way at last into the world.

Lily and her sisters arrived in the North on a brisk October day. Just outside the railroad station in New York City, they stood gaping at the street traffic and maze of buildings around them, June counting out the last of their expense money from Mr. Pastor, who'd said to take hackney cabs to his theater on the Bowery.

It had taken a while to make all the connections between the Double H Ranch and New York. There'd been the stage to San Antonio, and hardly a moment to spare before they'd had to brush off their clothes and prepare their jangled stomachs for the waiting coach to Houston. Then there'd been the railroad to Galveston. It was their first experience with a train, and although less jolting than a stagecoach, it had left them equally dusty and unsure on their feet. Next there'd been the steamboat to Charleston, and then an endless round of trains to New York itself.

Now, either June had been staring a moment too long at the few coins from the tiny reticule lying in her palm, or the Harper girls looked like awful greenhorns, because before even Lily could catch on, a gang of ragged boys lollygagging nearby raced over. In the wink of an eye they barreled through the group, leaving June with an empty hand.

She opened her mouth to scream, but Lily cut her short. "That'll be our first lesson about life in the big city, June. And probably a cheap one, at that." She turned to May standing stunned nearby. "You might want to grab that guitar case of yours before it disappears, too."

May grabbed as Lily took in the rest of them. Julie was ready to bawl, and March had lost most of her usual aplomb. They were all fed up.

"How are we going to get to Mr. Pastor's now, Lily?" April moaned. "We haven't a cent left to our names!"

"You oughtn't act so pale and frazzled, April. How'd you think Rick would feel? He'd expect you to show a little Texan fortitude." She swung around to the others. "We're supposed to be actresses, aren't we? Well, let's just show New York what kind of troupers the Harper Girls really are!"

"I really don't understand how—"

"Never mind, March. Just put out your arm for those hacks coming by."

The drivers stopped. "201 Bowery, please. Pastor's Opera House," Lily called up to each in turn. Then she shooed her sisters into the cabs.

"But, Lily," sniveled Julie from the seat next to her, "how will we pay the men?"

"Tony Pastor wanted us. Let Tony Pastor pay."

The great man himself was not at hand to receive his new stars, but a solicitous assistant paid their cab fares without batting an eye and escorted them to a nearby boardinghouse. He removed his hat while introductions were made to the lady of the house, a wizened old biddy named Mrs. Agatha Wallnut. Lily wasn't overwhelmed by either the ambience of the place or the possibilities inherent in taking all their meals with Mrs. Wallnut. Anyone that skinny couldn't possibly put out a good spread. And Lily was hungry. There hadn't been anything like a chile pepper or a decent hunk of steak since Galveston. It was clear nobody outside of Texas knew how to eat.

As the girls surveyed the front rooms of their new home, Arthur Riddle, the young assistant, stood by, fingering his beaver topper and glancing at the girls with shy eyes, like he wanted to ask them if it was all really true, what they'd done, but was too polite to inquire. Finally he made a move to leave, but stopped at the door. "Mr. Pastor is having the finishing touches put on your little play at this moment. I'll run it over to you as soon as it's ready in the morning. In the meantime, I wish you a pleasant good evening." He paused again, and finally closed the door behind him with reluctance.

Arthur Riddle's performance over, Lily turned to Mrs. Wallnut. "What's the schedule around here, missus?"

"Breakfast at eight, dinner at noon, and supper at six-thirty sharp. If you miss a meal, it's your own lookout." She consulted a timepiece decorating her bosom. "I'd best show you to your suite. It's getting past five already and the food to be seen after."

Mrs. Wallnut began climbing the stairs. "Mr. Pastor reserved the entire third floor for you. No guests after nine in the evening, and none beyond the parlor." She stopped to throw a beady-eyed glance back at May and the guitar case she clutched to her chest. "No noise after nine, either. I run a high-class establishment here, and I don't put up with no hanky-panky from theatrical types. And I don't care what type you be. I've seen 'em all come and go in the past twenty years, and that's God's truth."

Mrs. Wallnut proceeded up the stairs once more.

"I even put up with Chang and Eng, them Siamese twins Mr. Barnum had over at his museum before it burned to the ground last winter. Slept right here in my second-floor front parlor, they did, in the big double bed. Kept the whole house awake with their cantankerousness until I put my foot down. Even folks who's joined at the chest and been before the Queen of England herself can't get one over on Agatha Wallnut. There's a complete list of house rules writ out on your parlor table. I expect you to keep them, or you're out on the street with no refunds due."

It was a relief to turn the key on Mrs. Wallnut. The others

set down their burdens and explored, while Lily paused to contemplate the mysterious Siamese twins. It was a sobering thought to consider having to be tied for life to *any* of her sisters. But even Chang and Eng fled from her mind at June's shout of delight in finding their own indoor privy, complete with a tub and running water. Besides that, there was the small parlor and two adjoining bedrooms. But there were only two beds. Lily immediately staked out the parlor settee for her own accommodations. She wasn't tied to any of them yet, and had had enough of sharing with her sisters in jail, thank you.

Next she went to the double set of windows in the parlor and pushed up the sash of one to lean out. The sun was setting somewhere behind New York City, but durned if she could figure out where. All she saw was buildings. And such buildings. They were scrunched right one into the other, without a bit of breathing space. And the way they kept rising up, one story after the other, made a person giddy. If people wanted to live that high up, they ought to be finding some of the hills and buttes God had made for that purpose.

Just taking in the street made Lily hungry for the spaces of Texas and the Double H. It was getting cool out, too. It wouldn't be near this chilly yet back home. She shivered and pulled back into the room, shutting the window behind her.

Julie had thrown her bag in a bedroom and was wandering around the parlor, too. She watched Lily, who was now on her knees atop the green-flowered, threadbare carpet, inspecting the scarred lion heads at the foot of the settee.

"Do you think one of my samplers might brighten up the walls, Lily? Mama and I came up with a new saying just before we left home."

"What is it?"

" 'All the World's a Stage.' "

"Are you sure you didn't get that one from June?"

A gong rang through the house, reverberating all the way to the third floor.

"What's that?" April was emerging from the privy closet. Lily noticed that her eyes were red and swollen. She must be succumbing to homesickness, too. Who wouldn't after spending five minutes in this place?

"Maybe supper. If we're lucky, it might be edible. But I wouldn't take any bets on it."

The settee was lumpy, as lumpy as the dumplings at supper. And the boiled cabbage hadn't set too well, either. Lily tossed and turned and finally got up before dawn. Quickly braiding her hair, she slipped into the pants and shirt she'd snuck into her bag, and tiptoed down two flights of stairs. Outside, light was just beginning to color the sky. Working on instinct, Lily walked through the labyrinth of streets until she found a river and the sunrise. She sank down on the edge of a pier and gazed past the stick-like masts of ships to the east. At home she'd always had her own compass inside her head, and nothing could get her lost. Here she'd have to refigure everything, but she'd do it all right. Lily sat watching the river traffic slowly come to life, then, on suggestions from her rumbling stomach, navigated her way back to Mrs. Wallnut's.

It was midmorning before the promised script was delivered into their hands. The Harper girls draped themselves over the nearest bed and giggled for hours over what some hack writer had done to their true-life adventures.

The following morning they met Mr. Tony Pastor at last. They were guided into his cubbyhole office up behind the second balcony by Arthur Riddle. The girls swallowed up every remaining inch of space while they nervously examined the portly gentleman seated across the desk.

He, in turn, beamed upon them from behind an impressively waxed mustache and the fattest, longest cigar Lily had ever seen. It was even bigger than the ones Daddy had choked on after their trial.

"So. The Harper girls at last. Who'd have thought ones so young and innocent-looking could be so dangerous—especially at negotiations! I take my hat off to you, ladies."

He didn't really, because he didn't have one on to start with. But he did say it nicely. Mr. Pastor had a rich, resonant voice, probably from all the singing their landlady said he used to do before opening his own theater.

"So," he repeated, "what do you think of Pastor's Opera House? No saloon, or other deleterious surroundings. Nothing but high-class entertainments and quality audiences." He sucked at his cigar with evident pride. "Ready to get down to work?"

They nodded.

"Excellent. I'm assigning one of my people to you, to help you learn the ropes." He nodded to his assistant, who was still poking his head through the door. "Arthur, would you be kind enough to call in Miss Cordell?"

None of them had time to wonder over who Miss Cordell might be before a large, earthy woman made her entrance, reeking of carnation scent and dressed fit to kill in loud scarlet satins, which clashed with the curious orange-red of her frowzy hair.

Tony smiled. "Miss Cordell? The Harper girls."

Miss Cordell beamed. "My, ain't you a covey bunch. So young and innocent-looking!"

There it was again. The Harpers glanced at each other uneasily.

"Did I say something to set you off? Never mind, lovies, just come along with Tatty like good girls." She blew a kiss to Mr. Pastor. "I'll take care of 'em like they was my own."

Tony Pastor grinned around his cigar, and the Harpers filed out after the fascinating woman.

She led them down balcony stairs and up through the orchestra to the stage, breaking into a barrage of words as Mrs. Wallnut had done.

"Now we'll have to introduce ourselves proper like. My stage name is Camille Cordell. It was Tony's idea. He's such a darling man, but a little tightfisted nevertheless. You have to keep an eye out for him, you do. Not physically, dearies. He's not *that* kind of a man, thank goodness. But he has a good ear and never thought my christening name would make a proper go on the stage. You're so lucky to have a harmonious name like Harper. It will read well on the bills and broadsheets. Anyway"—she rattled on, with the Harpers drifting behind her, bug-eyed—"anyway, you may call me Tatty, which is what my dear old mother, may she rest in peace, always bellowed after me. It may have had something to do with our impoverished way of life, before I took to the stage. But Tatty I was, and Tatty I remain. Now then." They had reached the stage itself and were treading across its boards—tentatively, to say the least.

"Now then. Here we be. And only three days to make professionals of the lot of you."

Three days?

"Never fear, dearies. Tatty will give you aid and comfort. But first let me try and pick you out. The *Herald* articles were so exciting, and made you seem so real!" The girls were huddled together in front of the dimmed gas footlights. "Dear me. You, the one who is about to burst into tears. You must be the sensitive one, Julie. Goodness. We'll have to do something about that snood. They're not at all becoming enough for a actress on the stage."

Lily broke into her first grin that morning. Tatty was going to be all right, after all. As if reading her thoughts, the woman spun around. "And you're Lily, the tomboy. My, I wish I had such lustrous black hair. I'm afraid I've hennaed whatever I've got for so long I can't remember what it used to be."

And thus she continued with her identifications, getting everyone precisely correct, from March's haughty attempts at grandeur and April's Southern heart to May's musical pretensions and June's tight curls and desire for the stage. Lily figured

George Dunlop must have been a better writer than any one of them expected. It was too bad they hadn't read the articles themselves.

Under Tatty's tutelage, they began the next phase of their lives. There was a flurry of activity as they trod upon the boards in preparation for their two-a-day performances. Costumes were prepared, backdrops painted. Mr. Pastor even had broadsheets printed up to announce their opening. Lily was rather partial to them and made sure she got a bunch for souvenirs to take home. Daddy and Mama would certainly like one, and Ooh-long would prize it, no doubt. "The Harper Girls" definitely got top billing:

PASTOR'S OPERA HOUSE
Mr. Tony Pastor, proprietor and manager

This Saturday Afternoon and Evenings,
October 16–November 19,
will be performed by
THE HARPER GIRLS
in person,

YOUNG
AND
DANGEROUS!!

being their true-life adventures in the Wild West of Texas.
See them rob the stagecoach! See them incarcerated!
See them freed by justice!

RESERVED SEATS—50 CENTS   FAMILY CIRCLE—25 CENTS

Tatty and the other performers were slung in at the bottom of the broadsheet:

To conclude with the laughable sketch of
POST OFFICE SAM!
Messrs. SPAULDING, SPENCER, and MURPHY

K. Jarboe, Printer, 118 Broadway, New York.

As exciting as it was to see their names in print, opening day came too soon. Lily was scrunched in a dressing room backstage between her sisters, brushing down her britches before their first performance, running through the play in her head.

There were only four scenes, so they shouldn't mess them up too easily. And anyway, it was just like doing one of their old tableaux, only with a few words added. The first scene was all of them hanging around a painted backdrop of the Double H stable. While the stage designer had been painting that one, Lily had stood by to make sure he got a few things right, like the workbench with the branding irons and all. She'd even had him paint in some lounging chickens.

133

Well, all they had to do in this scene was stand or sit around talking about how poor Daddy was about to lose his ranch by foreclosure. That was easy enough. Then the writer had March come up with the robbery idea. It was too bad they couldn't give Daddy credit where credit was due, but that still had to remain a deep, dark secret, and anyway Lily was learning fast that what took place in a theater had little relationship to any living person or true fact.

She ran a cloth around her boots.

The second backdrop was the artist's conception of the desert, done without her supervision. Lily had had to make him add the butte after the fact; before that, it had just been filled with cactus and a few bleached cow skulls. For this scene, they had to run and change clothes fast—all except Lily, of course—and come out in trousers, with guns. Here Mr. Pastor had thrown caution and cost to the winds, as he put it, and hired a real coach, pulled by real horses, to clamber across the stage. There were only two of the horses, instead of six, but Lily figured what with tracking down a genuine stagecoach, Mr. Pastor had to cut costs somewhere. So they robbed the stagecoach, with Myron Long, the variety dancer, filling in as Ned Brewster. Spaulding and Spencer, the breakneck act, threw on U.S. Cavalry coats and glared out the coach windows. After dragging the bags and trunks offstage, the girls all had to rush to change for Scene Three, which found them languishing in jail.

Lily tucked in her shirt and faced the mirror to rouge up her cheeks, like Tatty had insisted was necessary so they didn't all look as if they had consumption on the other side of the stage lights.

It wasn't a jail like O.T.'s. They were on scruffy mats on the floor, and Mr. Pastor even had the stage manager let out some filthy rats to run across the stage. Lily had asked the stage manager how he expected to catch up with those rats after each show, but Jim Nixon only shrugged and said he could get a lifetime supply from the street arabs roundabout for a nickel a cageful, and a few more rats wouldn't change the opera house much. The rats, Lily decided, must be what some referred to as poetic license.

Anyhow, this was the scene Lily was proud of, because she'd added a bit of her own. They hadn't ever mentioned the file business to George Dunlop, since it hadn't seemed appropriate at the time. But it was Lily who had requested a file from Jim Nixon, so it was she who got to saw at the bars set into this backdrop, to the disgust of June and Julie. The others didn't seem to mind at all, though, especially May, because she got to plunk out her favorite melancholy Spanish tune on the guitar while the filing was commencing.

Lily checked her braid and pulled on her slouch hat.

Scene Four was the trickiest, as it had the most lines to say. It was set in the courtroom, with Myron Long, complete with ill-fitting beard, playing Judge Wiley. Spaulding stood in for the entire jury, and Spencer played their daddy, rejoicing over his daughters regained. Too bad Spencer was about a foot taller than Daddy, had a complete crop of hair, and had a bulging belly to boot.

There was a crisp knock at their dressing-room door. "Five minutes, ladies."

They all froze like statues. For at least a minute, until March broke the spell.

"Will you stop chewing on your braid, Lily Harper! It makes you look like you've never been fed a decent meal in your life!"

"It's almost cannibalistic," April added. "In fact, it even bothered me back in Texas, but there seemed no point in bringing it up there."

"I notice your fingernails seem to be chawed down to nothing, March," retorted Lily, "and you keep pulling at your nose, April. Course, if you want to behave like a passel of farm women out there on the stage—"

"Calm down," said June. "We're all nervous. In fact, my stomach feels fluttery like just before we robbed the stage-

135

coach, and Julie's gone green again. But we're going to ignore all that, just like we did before. We're going out there and do our best to make Daddy and Mama proud of us."

"And save the ranch," added Lily.

"That, too. We should stick together in this very special moment. Our first live audience!" June sighed with pleasure. "The first time for every one of us. We are the Harper Girls, after all!"

The rap at the door was harder this time.

"Curtain time!"

The Harper Girls gulped en masse and moved to meet their public.

The footlights were at their brightest now, and there were spotlights beaming down from somewhere up near the front balcony, too. Lily couldn't see beyond all those lights, wasn't sure there were real, live people on the other side of the stage, people who had actually come to watch *them*. There were some coughs, though, and the sound of persistent nose-blowing. She unfroze enough to begin going through the motions they'd rehearsed. It got a little easier. And then came roars of laughter, when June stopped the first scene by primping in her ragged gingham dress, pouting, and wondering out loud if *all* the robbery money had to be wasted on saving the ranch.

Lily was aghast. That part hadn't been written into the script. They were trying to prove how basically decent all of the Harpers were, after all. But June kept on primping, the audience kept loving it, and Lily knew then, without a doubt, that the ad-libbed additions would stay.

After that, it was hard keeping any of the Harpers back. Every time one of them got a laugh, or a smattering of applause, she just went and built on it. Another week of this, and Tony Pastor wouldn't recognize his original script.

When all of them were acquitted at the end of the courtroom

scene, the Harpers were called back on the stage four times for raucous applause. Standing there curtsying in the blinding light, Lily grudgingly had to admit to herself that there hadn't been anything quite like this back on the Double H. The audience seemed downright delighted with everything, in spite of their few flubbed lines. The Harpers found out how delighted when they tried to leave the opera house after the first matinee to run back to Mrs. Wallnut's in time for supper.

They left by the rear stage door, as they'd been instructed. At least, they tried to leave. Standing in the alley was a crowd of people, and when the Harpers showed their faces, the crowd rushed to meet them. March shoved her sisters back into the safety of the theater, slamming the door behind her.

"What's going on out there?" she gasped.

"Seemed near enough like a cattle stampede," volunteered Lily.

"What will we do?" Julie wailed. "I'm so tired and hungry!"

"We bull our way through."

"I could shove them out of the way with my guitar."

April gave Lily and May a warning look. "Nicely, please."

"Sillies!" June exclaimed. "They've come to admire us, and we must give them what they want. Graciously. Never forget that we are playing out their dreams." And pulling her cloak around her shoulders like an actress who'd taken the theaters of the world by storm, June wafted past her sisters to greet her adoring public.

The size of the crowd hadn't diminished. The rest of the girls pasted on delighted smiles and braved it. There were a number of very dashing young men-about-town done up in black tie, fancy waistcoats, and silk toppers, along with several smaller boys with mamas in tow and a band of old ladies. The young men clustered about June and March particularly, wanting to take them to private dinners; the boys wanted autographs from Lily and the rest; and the old ladies, apparently, wanted someone to castigate. The Harpers gave the autographs, refused the young men, and ran for their lives from the righteous, shouts of "Shame!" ringing in their ears. They didn't get back to the boardinghouse till most of the food was already gone.

With repetition, the novelty of their act diminished for the girls, proving a body could get used to anything—making moonshine, cattle rustling, stagecoach robbery . . . By the second week, Lily was thoroughly bored with it all. Even the applause at the end didn't move her like it had the first time. She'd as soon have been declaiming to a herd of Angus back on the ranch. Their lowing would have sounded about the same, too.

June was the only one who seemed to grow stronger and better with each dollop of applause. And she was the only one who could still face their alternately admiring and castigating stage-door public with equanimity. In fact, there was no keeping June down, onstage or off. She'd taken to wearing her blond hair in long, flowing, tight ringlets day and night, and constantly waltzed around in her stage mode, head so high Lily was afraid she was going to trip over something any moment and break her delicate nose, at the least.

It was nice, though, when they got their first week's pay for all that stage aggravation. It was the reason for being in New York, after all. In such a hullabaloo, it was fairly easy to forget that the Harpers were there, doing what they were doing, to save Daddy's ranch.

The hundred dollars came from Mr. Pastor's own hands, and they rushed back to their rooms to debate how exactly to handle it.

"Do you think it could be possible . . ." March asked from her seat at the table: "Do you think it could be possible that were this sent to Daddy, it might never get to the bank in San Antonio?"

Lily snorted. "There's nothing more possible, if you ask me."

The others had to agree. They were clustered around the

table, staring at the ten golden coins gleaming before them.

"What, then, might be the best arrangements to make with our money in the future? To see that the bills get paid?"

"And that we don't have to do *Young and Dangerous* for the rest of our lives," added Julie.

"Why don't we just send it direct to the San Antonio bank?"

"The perfect solution, Lily." March beamed. "But I have noticed the need for some spending money. Things we can't really ask Mr. Pastor to provide . . ."

"I lost my favorite needle," Julie commented. "And I surely would like another."

"I'd like to buy some of the piano sheet music everybody sells on the streets here. As a keepsake to take home, of course," added May.

"Tatty's been telling me that I ought to read up on Shakespeare and other great writers of the Theater, if I'm really serious about pursuing my career," said June from under the dinner plate she was balancing on her head to further improve her posture. "Books are expensive"—the plate slipped and crashed to the floor—"and easier to balance on one's head than Mrs. Wallnut's cheap china."

Lily admired the scattered bits of crockery now gracing the green rug. "Lucky Mrs. Wallnut wasn't hovering outside the door eavesdropping like she does on occasion. She'd hit you up dear if she knew you'd snuck that plate like you did." June bent carefully from the knees and began collecting the pieces. "As for me, I'd like bus fare to go clear up to this Central Park I heard mentioned. It's supposed to have sheep and everything. If I don't see some wide-open spaces soon, I'm going to bust."

March glanced at Lily. "Well then, would you approve, Miss Lily, if we subtracted a small amount for such purposes? It's not as if we were going to buy horribly expensive things for ourselves, like that wonderful bonnet I saw on the Ladies' Mile yesterday—"

"Why's everybody trying to play me for the bad guy? Seems

to me if we peel ten dollars off that hundred, and send the ninety to the bank directly, ain't nobody could complain."

"Done!" March banged the parlor table with her hand like a gavel. "One dollar walking money for each of us, each week. To be saved or spent entirely as we like. If Daddy asks, we can always call it for our hope chests." She looked around for confirmation and got it quickly. "And the other four we'll put by in a community pot for dire emergencies."

22

A letter from Daddy finally reached New York. He said Mama was fine, but sighing for each and every one of them. Rick was just back and fit to be tied to find his girl gone. Lily could almost hear Daddy chuckling through the scrawly lines of his writing: "Do him good to be missing April a little. Maybe it'll put a bee in his bonnet about arranging something a mite more permanent on her return. As for Tom, he headed back East from Abilene, like he promised his parents. So maybe you'd better start getting used to that idea, March. No point whatsoever in pining after what's not available."

Daddy also related news of Fredericksburg's first jailbreak. It seemed O. T. Williams had rounded up a serious confidence man from up North with a price on his head (not high, but a price nevertheless). Well, O.T. had slung the perpetrator in jail and headed down to the telegraph station to send the news. Then he'd gone to bed, a happy man, already figuring on how to spend his reward money. In the morning, the trickster was gone, apparently having filed through the bars of the entire back window overnight! O.T. was furious.

"I was wondering how long it would take till someone did that," Lily said, and they all laughed.

There wasn't that much more to the letter. Just Daddy saying how he missed them all, too, and was anticipating their return. And not to forget to send the money. Izzy had bought a new bull that would do wonders for the Double H's remaining cows.

"See there, I told you so," commented Lily. "That money would have never got near San Antonio. Although Daddy might have a point about renting Izzy's bull—" She stopped, as larger implications hit her. Maybe it was thinking on how hard the bull'd have to work to improve Daddy's stock. "Any of you begun figuring on what's going to happen after all of this theater business is finished? I mean, we'll maybe solve Daddy's money troubles, at least for the time being. But what about us? Can we just go back to what things were like before the robbery and the stage? What happens to our lives?"

March resettled herself in her uncomfortable chair with a groan. "You can't be referring to Tom, that villainous carpet-bagger, Lily."

"Don't go calling poor Tom a carpetbagger, March. He told you fair and square about his intentions long since. You just never believed he'd dally with you thataways, then take off for good."

March's face had gone pale, and April put a comforting arm around her shoulder. "Maybe he'll write, dear. He knew our ranch address, and Daddy could forward a letter easily enough."

March shrugged her off. "I don't notice your Rick writing!" She turned to May. "Nor Barly, either, for that matter. Then again, Barly probably doesn't know how to write."

"He does, too! He can read and write both! How do you

suppose he keeps track of all those wanted posters for O.T.?"

Julie broke off from her embroidery. "There's no point in fighting like this, sisters. I believe Lily meant to refer to the question of our reputation. Not so much the robbery business, at least in Texas, where most folks are on our side . . ." She frowned. "The longer we're on the stage, well . . . just take poor Tatty, the way people stare at her—and us—when we're out walking together before we've removed all our stage makeup. I've noticed fine ladies actually crossing the street so they don't have to brush past us, as if we had the Texas Fever or something . . ."

"And the way they mince as they do it," added April. She began mimicking the tight, tiny steps of fancy Eastern women, something her nature wouldn't have allowed her to do before her stage experience. "Can you imagine Mama ever walking like that? Or cutting a person for any reason?" She halted her demonstration across the rug. "Do you suppose Tatty's begun rubbing off on us adversely?"

"Don't you go putting down Tatty just because of her looks and broad experience," huffed Lily. "She's got a heart of gold!"

"You've no concept of what a broad experience really means, Lily," March said. "You're only thirteen."

"I know enough about it to steer you away from all them free midnight suppers being offered, sure enough, Miss March! Being offered to near all of you, even June, who's still only fifteen, no matter how old she tries to act!"

"Sisters, please!" Julie was neatly packing up her stitchery. "It's almost time for our next show. We should carry these things in our hearts for a while, and not resort to broad farce, as this is working toward."

June beamed admiringly at her sister. "You're taking to the theater better than I ever expected, Julie. Even catching on to stage language! There's hope for you yet."

Lily still couldn't sleep right in New York. Strange street sounds came filtering through the third-floor windows all night. There were the usual carriages, and the voices of men sauntering home from the corner saloon at all hours, sometimes singing, sometimes fighting. Around dawn came the milkman, and the peddlers setting up their sidewalk carts for the day's business. She continued rising extra early and exploring the streets. She'd get back in time for breakfast, then disappear again till dinnertime at noon. There wasn't much else to be done before their first show in the afternoon.

Her sisters settled into a different pattern. Without exception, they'd taken to skipping breakfast. They were lighter eaters anyway, and preferred to sleep late, rising only in time for lengthy beautifying sessions before the noon meal. No matter how noble the intentions they'd voiced, most of them took to squandering their weekly allowances on various face creams, perfumes, and unguents. That was fine with Lily if that was what they wanted. Herself, she was saving as much of the money as possible. She'd been hanging around the livery and saddlery places and had spotted a saddle that would do Checkers truly proud. It would take a lot more weeks to come up with the price, though.

Normal frustrations aside, according to Mr. Pastor the Harpers were doing just fine. They had a meeting with him one afternoon at the beginning of their fourth week in New York.

"Well, girls," he said expansively, twirling a waxed mustache end and beaming at them from behind his usual cigar. "Much as I'd like to extend your stay here with us, I've been getting some good offers to represent you on the road."

"What kind of a road?" Lily was already skeptical. True, Tony Pastor had been more than fair with them, holding up to every piece of what he'd offered, right down to room and board and costumes. Still, she wouldn't mind at all checking over the daily receipts from his opera house, although June could make more sense of them than she could. It seemed like they'd been playing to practically full houses nearly every show. And if you figured fifty cents times four or five hundred people, twice a day, that left a fair piece of profit for Mr. Pastor, even if you took into account his overhead costs.

He smiled again. "I had in mind a few places like Wilmington, followed by Baltimore and Washington City. Then maybe down to Charleston. I think you'll go over well in the South—"

"Would that be Wilmington, Delaware?" It was March, of course.

"It would, indeed. It's the only Wilmington that counts, theatrically."

"How long would we stay there?"

"A week in each location would be suitable. That's about the usual run for special productions in the provinces."

"What would happen after Charleston?" Homesickness was shining from Julie's eyes.

"Well, there'd be no point in wasting further opportunities on the way home, would there? I've had expressions of interest from New Orleans, Houston, and San Antonio, too. That would round your tour out and end you up in home territory. In fact, should it work to everyone's advantage, I just might consider organizing some other talent to follow your show in the same places. A sort of little circuit, managed by Tony Pastor of New York . . ." He leaned back in the chair behind his desk, obviously pleased with his idea.

June waved away a cloud of smoke. "So exactly what does that guarantee us?"

"That would be, let me see. Wilmington, Baltimore . . ." He started counting off on his fingers. "Seven more weeks of work, at seven hundred dollars total. Not forgetting I'm covering your travel, room, and board all the way back, just like we agreed. That's quite a concession, I hope you realize. Normal players, they just cover all that themselves." He glanced shrewdly at June. "However, should you consider that theatrical life appeals to you—and I have noticed it seems to, Miss June—well, should that be the case, I might be able to use you in the future. I'm thinking besides of putting together a road show of *The Black Crook*, and could use a juvenile, or possibly even an ingenue . . ."

At the mention of the word "ingenue," June lit up. "Could you really, Mr. Pastor?"

"We'll discuss that later, privately, June," March interrupted. "For now, we might be interested in your plan, Mr. Pastor. But not at the same rate as here in New York. We aren't amateurs anymore. We've proven ourselves. A slightly larger recompense would be in order." She paused. "Say, double? We haven't finished paying off our daddy's debts yet."

"I certainly would like to meet this daddy of yours someday," muttered Tony Pastor. He got down to negotiations.

 Lily had hoped Wilmington would be different from New York. It wasn't. A little less crowded, of course, but it was still a big old ugly Eastern city. Even the sagging buildings of their own spread would look good after all this.

Mr. Pastor had indeed sent the whole show on the road. That meant they'd still have Myron Long and Spaulding and Spencer to fill in during their scenes. It also meant they had Tatty with them.

All along, Tatty had been a delight and a help, but she'd also been more. Every time March got to thinking black thoughts about Tom Carter and looked more appraisingly at those young gents by the stage door, Tatty had come along out of nowhere and wafted the lot of them off to safety. "You've got plenty of time for oysters on the half shell when you're as old as me, dearies," was all she'd ever say.

It got so that Lily had built up a strong desire to taste oysters. She'd finally done so one of their last days in New York, at a tiny shack down by the wharves along the East River. Her mouth puckered now at the thought of that slithery, cold mass sliding down her throat. As far as she was concerned, she'd be happy to forgo any further acquaintance with the beasts forever.

Their new Wilmington boardinghouse held no surprises. More cabbages and lumpy dumplings on the table, and more worn carpeting and peeling wallpaper. But they didn't have as much time to bemoan this selection. They were on a tight schedule now, and were settled in barely in time for their first show. The show itself went all right, but Lily did notice that March was becoming more and more distraught as their play proceeded. She kept gazing wistfully out over the footlights, and by the time she stood up to do her speech for the trial, there were real tears on her face and anguish in her voice. The audience loved it, and March got a solo curtain call. She didn't relish it the way June would have.

Nevertheless, there was a surprise waiting for March when they got back to the dressing room. Somebody had sent her a bunch of flowers. Now, they'd gotten a few bouquets from gentlemen back in New York, and once even a bottle of champagne, which Tatty had instantly removed to save them from "temptation and degradation," as she'd put it, hugging the bottle to her bosom. But they hadn't expected anything of the sort here. March pushed them all aside to open the card. "It's from Tom!"

"What does he say?"

"Is he coming to see us?"

At that point, all of them would welcome a face from home.

"It doesn't say. Anything. Just 'Tom' . . ."

Still and all, March got changed in double time and was the first at the stage door. "Now, don't go making a fool of yourselves, any of you. If he's here." She eyed her youngest sister. "You, especially, Miss Lily. We don't want him to think we're forward."

"A fine time it is to be worrying about appearing forward, March. After all them evenings you spent out checking fences with Tom back home on the Double H."

"Hush up, Lily. That's the little you know about courting!"

"I don't want to know any more at all if it puts a body in such a dither as Tom does you. And besides, maybe he's not out there at all. If I was his fancy parents, I'd have him locked up till we move on to Baltimore."

"Please, Lily!" It was April. "Try to control yourself. This is very important to March."

"All right."

But then he wasn't there at all. Just the usual miscellaneous crowd, except they seemed to have left the moralizers behind in New York.

Lily glanced at March's face, then wished she hadn't. Fed up as she was, heartbreak wasn't something she wished on her oldest sister.

March changed her strategy after that. She got up as early as Lily the next morning, and carefully prepared her best dress.

"What are you up to, then?"

"I've decided to take a tour of the banking establishments of Wilmington."

"You can't do that, March! You can't throw yourself at Tom thataways, and embarrass him to boot. It ain't fair."

"This has nothing to do with fairness, Miss Lily. It's war! Besides, I believe our financial situation could use some learned counseling. I'm just going to inquire about intelligent investments."

"You got nothing to invest."

"I might, if I saved my weekly allowance. Besides, the bankers don't have to know the entire truth of my capital worth."

Lily shook her head. She could go and wake Tatty, but Tatty would only insist on going along with March, which would make the situation even worse. To a staid city like Wilmington, Mr. Pastor's troupe, off the stage, might just as well have recently landed from the moon.

March went anyway, and Lily followed, from a decent distance. The first two banks were apparently the wrong ones, but when March didn't emerge from the third after five minutes, Lily slipped out of the shadows and went inside.

It wasn't at all like the bank in Fredericksburg. For one thing, there was shiny, polished marble all over the place. For another, there were liveried guards sprouting from behind every potted palm. The guards made Lily slightly nervous, and also glad she hadn't worn her ranch clothes that morning.

It took a moment to pick her sister out, but she was there, all right. Sitting behind a fancy mahogany railing, in earnest conversation with a young man Lily had never seen before. Or had she? Lily squinted across the lobby's expanse of marble, from behind a huge, ornamental urn, then gulped. It couldn't ever be Tom, could it?

She marched across the floor, directly up to the railing. There a sign sitting on his desk proclaimed for all the world: *Thomas Carter, Jr., Vice President*. But Tom himself was sorrowfully changed. He was crammed into a dull-black frock coat, with high collar and necktie. His wavy hair had been trimmed and slicked down, and he'd already begun losing the bronze of the Texas hills from his face.

"Tom!"

The lovers looked up.

"If there's one thing I can't abide, it's a sneak and a snake," March hissed. "What are you doing here?"

148

Lily didn't flinch. "Simmer down, March. There's people listening."

And there were. Disapproving faces glanced over from the cashier booths. Tom rose, displaying discreetly striped gray trousers over discreetly buffed black shoes. Sissy shoes, nothing like his good sturdy boots from his days at Izzy Henry's place. Lily opened her mouth to comment on his sad downfall, but was ushered into his cubicle and shushed instead.

"For heaven's sake, Lily," Tom said. "This isn't the time or place—"

"Where is, then? And when? You've got poor March in such a tizzy, she can't hardly concentrate on her lines. The least you could've done was write—"

"You think I like it here?" he burst out, trying to keep his voice down. "You think this is my idea of how to spend the rest of my life? I've been home little more than a week and haven't had a moment's peace yet. They won't let me near the land and racing stock. I've got to get dressed up to come into the bank each morning. Then I have to sit behind this desk looking ridiculous, and trying to make believe I'm doing something useful. After that I have to go home and dress up worse for dinner and the round of social events I walked back into. I'd trade it all for your daddy's broken-down ranch anyday."

March brightened. "Would you really, Tom?"

"Well, maybe not your daddy's place exactly, but there's a big piece of land up to the north that's for sale—we passed through it on the drive up to Kansas—and with a little bit of capital—"

Tom never finished what he was trying to say. A large, silver-haired man dressed in the same banker's getup was suddenly standing outside the cubicle. "I trust this is banking business you're carrying out, young man."

Tom blanched. "I've just had a surprise visit from some old Texas friends, Father. May I introduce you to the Harper girls, March and Lily?"

Hah, Lily thought with satisfaction. His father wasn't ever a "Pop." She watched the elder Carter take in the two of them, from their genteel, subdued clothing to March's face, scrubbed clean as a plate from any theatrical makeup. Two little red spots emerged on March's cheeks nevertheless.

"That would be the same Harper girls currently playing at the Odd Fellows' Hall, wouldn't it."

All three nodded. Old man Carter exploded. "How could my only son consort with notorious felons and *actresses* in my bank! We'll discuss this directly, after these, these . . . are escorted out." Then he merely inclined his head, and two security guards came at a run.

"Now, just a minute here, sir!" The insult smarted badly on Lily. "We ain't either of us felons! We were acquitted fair and square and wouldn't ever even consider robbing your old bank. Banks were never in our line, anyhow."

The guards were bristling. Tom was leaning over the desk, whispering frantically to March. "I never intended any of this, March, believe me! I come into my trust fund next year, and—"

"We won't be in Wilmington next year, Tom Carter. We'll only be here for five more days. If you want to discuss this any further, you know where to find us. At the theater! Although I'm not sure there remains anything to discuss. After all, it was a *banker*"—she spat out the word as if it was dirty—"a *banker* who placed my sisters and me in this untenable position to begin with."

The two Harpers marched out of the bank with heads high, ignoring the escorts to either side of them. It wasn't until they were back in the safety of their rented room that March let go. She threw herself onto the nearest bed, knocking over the array of makeup and unguents May and June had laid out there to play with. Then the tears came.

Tom was waiting by the stage door after their evening performance. He was dressed up fit to kill, with a silk topper and

150

everything. His arms were filled with roses and a very expensive box of chocolates. March sailed right past him. So did four of the remaining Harper sisters. Lily pulled up the rear. She divested Tom of his burdens, then looked him briefly in the eye. "You'll have to go one better than this, Tom Carter." Then she picked up her skirts and ran after the others.

Tom was waiting the rest of the nights, too. On every one of them, his arms were filled with more flowers and candy. And on every night, March ignored it all, to run back to the boardinghouse and collapse in tears. Things got so bad Lily was overjoyed to pack her things and move down the line to Baltimore. Also, she couldn't face another chocolate for a while.

Tatty had gotten fed up on singing old Civil War songs like "Can I Go, Dearest Mother?" and "Bear Gently, So Gently, the Roughly Made Bier." Besides, she must have figured that since Baltimore was probably south of the Mason-Dixon Line, her Northern songs might get booed off the stage. Accordingly, she added several recent novelty numbers to her repertoire, including "Oil on the Brain" and "The Flying Trapeze." The "Trapeze" number went over particularly well, with Tatty swinging by her arms from a trapeze let down from the flies. The gentlemen of the audience seemed to enjoy the element of surprise as her skirts went ballooning up into the air on each swing, and took to egging her on to higher acrobatic feats. Tatty enjoyed the extra attention, and supplemented it by donning red silk bloomers beneath her voluminous skirts.

Lily was admiring her friend's performance from the wings on their third day in Baltimore. *Young and Dangerous* was finished for the moment, and there wasn't a whole lot more to do. Baltimore had turned out to be a smelly town, filled with factories whose smokestacks fed a thick, black smoke into the skies at any moment of the night or day. The air had already set the delicate Julie into coughing spasms, and Lily decided it was best to be out of it entirely. But that left her completely at loose ends. She was used to being always busy at something from her days on the ranch, helping to fill in for all the hired help Daddy never could afford.

It was all this infernal *waiting* a body had to do in the theater that put her off the most. Waiting to go onstage, waiting between scenes, waiting till it was time to pack up and move on again. If she'd had a piece of harness in her hands to fiddle with and polish up, it might not have been so bad. May had her guitar to console her, and Julie her endless stitching. For herself, Lily was just plain about to die from all the waiting.

Their overall situation hadn't changed much from Wilmington. March was still in a state of total desolation over Tom. She'd gone from pure anger at him to castigating herself for refusing to speak to him or even acknowledge his peace offerings. She now went through her role on the stage like an automaton, then returned to their boardinghouse to shut herself up in bed for the remainder of her waking hours. It tended to cast a pall over everything and everyone: a pall deeper than the blighted Baltimore air.

Lily sighed. Things couldn't go on like this. Not for the next eight or nine weeks it would take them to get back home to the Double H. Especially with Christmas coming on.

It would be their first Christmas away from Mama and Daddy, and it was mighty disheartening to think that they wouldn't be all together, with special cookies and cakes to bake, and maybe the first snows of the season to dust the rangeland, and Mama reading about the Nativity like she always did on Christmas Eve, with the whole family warming around the fireplace heaped up high with mesquite and juniper roots and anything else they could find to burn . . .

There was a burst of raucous applause as Tatty swooped down to earth at the finish of her number. Then Tatty was edging right into Lily as she blithely tripped off the stage. She was all smiles of pleasure and exertion, reeking of carnations like a Bowery flower peddler's cart.

"What is it, dearie? Was I that outrageous?"

"No, Tatty. You were wonderful, as usual. Can't you hear them still clapping? They'd like an encore."

Tatty sniffed. "I'm sure they would, but I've given my all to the matinee crowd for this day. Besides, the orchestra hasn't any more of my sheet music. Did you hear how they flubbed the second chorus just now? I do wish Mr. Pastor would send his own musicians with us in future." She stopped to consider Lily again. "Come help me with my buttons, sweetie. You're looking down at the mouth."

Back in her dressing room, Tatty lit one of her slim black cigarettes and inhaled with pleasure as Lily began on the score of tiny buttons down the actress's back. Lily's eyes slipped to the notice posted next to Tatty's mirror.

Front Street Theater, Baltimore
WARNING: *The Following Words Are Forbidden to Be Used in This Theater:*
slob, sucker, damn, hell, socks, nuts

It was a curious list of words, and she'd noticed the same or similar cautions in dressing rooms from New York to Baltimore. Just one more of the curious things she'd seen since that day O.T. had drug them off to his jail. The last few months had been what some might consider an education in itself. That thought pleased Lily, and she broke into a smile.

"Now, that's better," Tatty said. "Considerably so. You want to tell Tatty what's got you so down? Aside from your big sister and her romantic entanglements? She should have known better than to set her heart for the gentry, poor dear. They never pan out like good honest working folk."

"Oh, Tatty." Lily gave her a hug. "You're such a nice thing. I'd love to have you meet up with Mama and Daddy and see our ranch, and my horse Checkers—"

"Why, Lily, I do believe you, of all your sisters, has come down homesick. Well, I suppose it is getting nigh onto Christmas. That's traditionally a difficult time for show people. Always trying to remember the homes we never had." She smiled gently. "And do you really believe your sainted mama would approve of me? With all my wicked ways?"

"You never could be wicked, Tatty! It's just your style of living—the smoking and the occasional bottle of wine, and, well, we each of us has different ways. That's one thing I've learned on this trip."

"Then you've learned more than most in a lifetime, Lily. My, but if I'd had a daughter of my own, I think I would've liked it to be you."

Lily gave her another hug, then rubbed at her eyes. "Do you think we might be able to do something special for Christmas? On the road like we are?"

"Christmas. That would put us somewhere . . . let's see, probably just past Charleston, on the way to New Orleans. And yes, of course we can do something special. Even on a steamboat. Blow your nose like a good girl and finish those buttons. We'll be missing our suppers at the boardinghouse."

A letter from Daddy had caught up with them that same day in Baltimore, between supper and the evening show. March was propped up on pillows in bed, her supper tray before her, empty. At least her broken heart hadn't kept her from eating.

Now she bestirred herself to read the letter aloud. "Daddy

says, and I quote, 'It's all fine and good you girls have taken to paying off the bank in San Antone so serious like, but things ain't great here, either.'" She turned the page. "Apparently he's running low on winter oats for the horses, not to mention staples for the kitchen, and the ranch-house roof is leaking cold drafts like nobody's business now that winter is upon them."

The sisters absorbed this in silence.

"Rick has offered to help repair the roof if Daddy gets in the supplies, and apparently Ooh-long has been missing Lily to the extent of riding over with delicacies for Mama. Mama wishes we'd come home soon, because she's uncomfortable trying to keep up a conversation with him. Also, she has to eat what he brings to be polite, but heathen food doesn't agree with her stomach."

"How far are we from paying off the bank in San Antonio, June?" Lily asked.

From a pocket hidden within the folds of her skirt June whipped out the small account book. "We sent $360.00 from New York City, and another $90.00 last week when we left Wilmington. That plus the $100.00 we paid from Fredericksburg adds up to $550.00. That means we can close off that debt this week, just barely making the foreclosure deadline, and send the other $40.00 to the Fredericksburg bank against Daddy's account there."

"What about our hope-chest money?" The raise March had negotiated from Mr. Pastor for their work on the road amounted to sixty dollars a week, ten for each of them.

"Lily," March said sternly, "we've got to be hard about that, or Daddy will bleed us dry. I just know he will. Having that is our only chance for a little independence once we get back home."

Lily accepted the truth morosely. "Well then, I vote we send our 'dire emergency' money to Daddy. How much should there be of that, June?"

June checked her book. "Twenty-four dollars as of this week in Baltimore. But that will leave us without any sort of a cushion if we're supposed to save our hope chest funds."

"It don't sound like Daddy and Mama got much of a cushion, either. How do you suppose Daddy managed before we took to bringing in money?"

"Loans from usurious bankers," hissed March, with vengeance. "He borrowed money from the lowest creatures on God's earth."

"They can't be that low if they kept us all on the Double H for this long, March. Seems to me you're dramatizing the situation somewhat."

"You can still say that, Lily, after having been in Thomas Carter, Jr.'s bank in Wilmington?"

"Well, I guess maybe the Eastern banks might be in the moneymaking business, what with all that marble and stuff they have flung around. Still—"

"There!" Julie interrupted. "I've outlined my newest piece. What do you all think of it? It's the first saying I've come up with on my own, without a consultation with Mama." With a flourish she held up her latest: **NEITHER A BORROWER NOR A LENDER BE.**

25

The train for Washington City was leaving in an hour, but Lily and her sisters estimated they had enough time to stop at the closest bank to the station to get the coins and bills in their pockets changed into a money order for Daddy. Tatty was left in a rented carriage, guarding their trunks with a rolled-up umbrella as the girls piled out in front of the bank building.

March turned around as they gathered behind her. "You know, it needn't take all six of us to accomplish this task, sisters."

"It's our emergency money being sent, March," commented June as she hunted in her reticule for the account book. "It's our right to oversee the transaction."

March got defensive. "You're sure you're not all just trying to keep me from making a fool of myself again, knowing my true feelings about such establishments?"

"Really, March," said April. "It's not Tom's bank we're going into. I'm sure we all expect you to act with complete decorum."

After a brief glance toward the heavens, March gathered herself to push open the heavy door. A bank guard hovering on the other side unexpectedly performed the service and the Harper girls swept in.

They lined up for one of the several busy bank tellers and began rummaging for their last-minute contributions. Leaning against another of those huge marble urns that seemed to be standard decorations for Eastern bank lobbies, Lily pulled from her pocket a quarter—the last of her weekly spending money, which she'd decided virtuously to add to the amount. She suddenly noticed a ruckus starting up amongst the people in front of March, and stood on tiptoe to peer over the bodies blocking her view. The teller's face had gone a pasty gray.

"What in tarnation's going on up there?" She'd said it to no one in particular, and barely had it out when something was shoved into the small of her back.

"What the . . . ?" Lily spun around to find a masked man behind her, the mask being a vast woolen muffler drawn up over his nose, whisks of a large mustache puffing it out in curious directions. The rest of him was nattily dressed in the latest gentlemen's fashions.

"Shut your trap, young lady, and hand over that money in your hand. This here is a holdup." With his free hand, he reached for the coin clutched in her fingers. "And hand over anything else of value, too."

Lily clung to her quarter stubbornly. "You got a ranch being foreclosed or something? From the cut of your trousers, it don't look like it."

"Cut the small talk, kid. I and my partners are professionals." He poked her with his weapon again, this time in the stomach. "Now give!"

"Please don't upset the gentleman, Lily!" It was Julie, eyes as wide as they could go.

The diversion gave Lily time to look about. Up front, her assailant's accomplice, similarly attired, turned from the teller to wave his gun at Lily's sisters and the other customers standing behind him. The customers were all scared silly. At the door, a third robber had a gun trained on the guard who'd let them in.

Lily saw red. Someone was trying to steal the money they'd worked so hard to earn—even the last quarter in her hand. The fact that she was now standing in the other shoe—in Ned

Brewster's boots, so to speak—hardly crossed her mind. The only thing apparent was that a masked villain was before her, pointing a handsomely tooled Colt revolver at her chest. And he didn't even have a proper reason for robbing the bank, dressed up as swank as he was.

"Nuts to this, and socks, too!" Lily didn't even know what she intended to do, but in her righteous anger she unintentionally rammed into the urn she'd been lounging against. Then she backed off to stare. It was rocking back and forth on its pedestal, hypnotizing both herself and her assailant. The arc became wider, until with a graceful swoop the urn toppled smack onto the robber's well-polished boot. Astonished, he opened his mouth in a silent scream. His revolver dropped to the floor, and he followed.

Lily bent and snatched up the gun. It felt good to have a firearm there again, the kind that'd been standard Civil War issue for officers, according to Rick, who always carried one like it out on the range for shooting at rattlesnakes. Now it was pointed down at the stomach of a different kind of snake.

"Move back, and get your hands up to the sky, varmint!" The man sprawled on the floor and whimpered.

Her sisters were flabbergasted.

"Lily! What are you doing?"

"Hush up, May. I'm just protecting our hard-earned money."

Julie tried, too: "But, Lily, those other men . . ."

The robber by the door had dropped his attention from the guard and was aiming in Lily's direction. Lily pointed the Colt and let off a round. She gasped at the forgotten recoil, but her target was in worse shape. His weapon fell as he let out a high-pitched screech, did a backwards dance, and grasped his wounded hand, only to cry out louder.

"What are you waiting for?" Lily yelled at the cowed guard. "Pick up that weapon!" Then she whirled around and found out why the guard had been cowed. The robber in front, in a last-ditch effort to save the debacle, had his free arm around

March's waist, hauling her up close as a shield, and he was prodding April with his revolver.

"Don't you dare hurt them!" yelled June as she flung herself at the man.

June was easily cast aside. "Get on the floor, all of you," he snarled. "Especially you with the gun. And don't move!"

Lily estimated that if anyone was going to get shot, it was her, the way that gun was waving between April and herself as the other customers dropped. Well, she was fed up on the stage anyway. And Texas seemed like so far away she'd likely never see it again.

Without blinking, she tightened both hands around the revolver and aimed, straight and true, for the nearest trousered leg. It was a good six inches from March's skirts, so she didn't figure on hurting her big sister any. She pulled the trigger and guessed she'd hit a bull's-eye, because the robber suddenly tore away from March and smashed back into the wall of the cashier's cubicle, yelling, "My knee! She got my knee!"

But Lily wasn't really listening. She was too busy letting out a blood-curdling Rebel yell, and a few other things her sisters reminded her about later. Then she was twirling around, searching for any other assailants to shoot at. Catching a movement from the robber by the door, she let off another round in his direction, just to put a little more fear into him.

After this, Lily allowed herself a satisfied glance at her Colt. It was truly amazing, the kind of power that could be gotten out of a .44 caliber bullet. It'd been like a steam engine ramming into those bandits, even just winged like they were.

Unfortunately, her first assailant wasn't as subdued as she'd thought. He rose suddenly on his good foot and tackled Lily from the side. Lily tried to aim the gun, but he grabbed the barrel and wrestled it from her hand, landing a tremendous blow on her eye. He was much stronger than anyone duded up like a swell ought to be. She reached for the Colt again, and this time it crashed into her jaw. Didn't he know he was taking unfair advantage over a female? Didn't these Northern criminals have any sense of honor? No wonder the South had lost the War.

That war at least.

"Get away from my little sister, you brute!" March's voice registered on Lily as five Harpers converged to attack Lily's assailant like vicious mountain lions, scratching and biting . . .

By the time Tatty barged into the bank, umbrella at the ready and the police on her heels, the robber had stopped struggling. As the other customers got shakily to their feet, Tatty and the police pulled apart the pile, one by one. Lily was found at the bottom, under her tormentor, bruised, but hanging on to the gun and grinning.

"I thought you girls were just going to send some money to your daddy," their friend said.

May found her voice first, only a few octaves too high. "We truly tried, Tatty, but these villains wanted to *steal* it!"

"Can you imagine!" June was all outraged innocence as she tried to pat her curls into a semblance of order.

Tatty poked the sharp point of her umbrella into the chest of Lily's robber, who'd been hauled to his feet by the police. His muffler had been pulled off to reveal bristling mustaches and chin whiskers around a grimace of a mouth.

"It was supposed to be a clean, simple job," he muttered with disgust. "Before these, these—"

"These *Harper Girls* come up against you," filled in Tatty with pride. "Serves you right. The Harpers ain't no Eastern wilting lilies. If you'd caught our show at the Front Street Theater, you'd have known better. Are you all right, girls?"

By now Lily was dusting herself off, too. "Never better, Tatty. Maybe Baltimore's not such a bad place after all."

The Harper girls missed their train to Washington. It took a while for the police to sort things out, and then the sisters insisted on completing the transaction they'd come for. The president of the bank himself did the honors for them, even though he'd closed down the bank to any other patrons for the rest of the day. When he suggested that a modest reward might be in order, Lily requested the Colt revolver of her assailant, who turned out to be Big Frank McCoy, along with his gang of "bank burglars." Lily got what she wanted, along with fifty dollars cash money, too.

Trying as they were to catch the next train so they wouldn't miss their first evening show, the Harpers had bumbled through the newspaper reporters waiting for them outside the bank in Baltimore.

The telegraph worked quicker than the trains, though, and a fresh batch of reporters was waiting for them at the B&O Station in the capital. The Harpers were bombarded with questions, and Lily got to show off her prize revolver. It was a duded-up version of Rick's—complete with ivory grips, silver plating, and ornate engravings. An artist from *Harper's Weekly* was also at hand to do a quick sketch of Lily in appropriate shooting pose, complete with rapidly puffing eye, although he passed on the loose tooth she wiggled for him. Lily was ready to give in to the cries for a demonstration of her shooting abilities when March and Tatty intervened.

"Really, Lily! You're making an undue spectacle of yourself!"

"Is that because they're paying more attention to me than to you, March?"

"Now, girls," interrupted Tatty, "normally I'd approve of such publicity, as it can't but improve our show attendance. However, in this case we are too close to missing the show itself. And that wouldn't do. No, it wouldn't do at all."

"Haven't we got enough reason for it, Tatty?"

"Reason or not, Lily, the stage manager will dock us for unprofessional behavior if we're late."

"Can he do that, Tatty?" June asked.

"He most certainly can."

162

Without further ado, the Harper entourage collected their trunks and rushed to their next opening night.

They were still in Washington several days later when they received another missive from Mr. Pastor. The publicity and standing-room-only crowds at their shows ever since the foiled bank robbery must have impressed him:

CONGRATULATIONS BALTIMORE COUP STOP PROUD OF ALL ESPECIALLY LILY STOP REQUESTS POURING IN OTHER CITIES STOP NEW IMPROVED CONTRACT FOLLOWS STOP ADDITIONAL BANK SCENE READY AFTER SAN ANTONIO ENGAGEMENT STOP WE'RE GOOD FOR ANOTHER TWO YEARS BEST REGARDS PASTOR

Lily groaned as March read the news. Her body still throbbed in remembrance of her recent beating, all over. She'd arrived at the theater late again, and was bent over the washbasin, trying to freshen up. Her tongue was back to worrying that loose tooth, another souvenir of natty Big Frank. She surely hoped it wouldn't fall out. There weren't any more coming to fill the gap. Then again, she had always mightily admired those gold teeth of Ooh-long's. Would a person have to go clear to China to find one of those?

"Are you with us, Lily?" April asked.

Her tongue slipped back into her mouth and she pulled away from the basin, holding a grubby wet cloth to her black eye. A nice raw steak would've been best for the eye. Daddy always said there was nothing like a piece of a good cow to fix all your ills.

May gave her a poke. "Lily, did you hear that telegram?"

"I guess so." Lily rearranged the cloth on her face. "But I don't want to think about it. Our tour has certainly had its interesting moments, but I never meant to make a life's work out of it. I'm ready to head home."

"We all of us want to go home, Lily. But the extra money . . ." April pulled out a long-awaited letter from Rick that had been forwarded to their Washington lodgings. It was already worn thin from constant handling. "With what Rick says he's saved, and another few months of this, why, he might even be able to leave Mr. Henry's and buy us a small spread of our own."

That they'd been discussing the telegram at length before Lily's arrival became apparent.

"There's nothing that will coerce me into continuing on the stage further," Julie stated quietly but definitively.

June turned from primping at the mirror. "The extra exposure could only help with my career."

"And I wouldn't have to be stuck at the Double H with only Tom on my mind," March said.

"We're not making a decision on it yet," May interjected. "And when we do, it ought to be a vote, fair and square. And not till the last of our engagements, in San Antonio. Besides, I don't think Barly would approve." She picked up her guitar and began tuning it, as if the discussion were closed.

But Julie opened it up again. "May's right about voting, but it ought to be a secret vote, not just talking things over like we've done before."

"It needn't be secret to know what you'd vote!"

"Now just a minute, June—"

Lily glanced at her squabbling sisters with her one good eye. If it came to that, it would be a hard vote, split right down the middle like they seemed to be at present. But vote they'd have to, if only to keep them from tearing out each other's hair. The sharp rap on the door saved her from further considerations.

"Curtain time, ladies!"

Sometimes it came in handy that the show had to go on.

26

☞ Most of the purple had disappeared, but Lily's left eye was still tinted yellow by Christmas. At least her front tooth had tightened up, leaving the question of a gold one like Oohlong's to the future.

They celebrated the holiday in the salon of the *Cotton Queen*, four hours out of Charleston. Tatty had gone all out trying to cheer up the girls. The Baltimore adventure went far toward taking March's mind off Tom, but the euphoria of the publicity, and the pleasure of knowing they'd all pitched in for each other when it counted, couldn't last forever. Especially since they were so far from home for the holiday.

Most of the salon had been reserved for the Tony Pastor troupe, and Tatty cajoled Myron Long and Spaulding and Spencer into dressing up like the Three Kings. She chose the role of Mary for herself, with Hilton Murphy standing by as Joseph. George Swaine played the donkey with good nature, in between introducing the act with his banjo. The whole production would have been a smashing success if the choppy seas hadn't turned stormy off Beaufort.

Just at the point where the Kings were set to make their offerings of treasure, the whole ship lurched something terrible to one side. Lily and her sisters were jumbled into each other from their salon seats in the audience, and had hardly gotten untangled when they were shoved in the opposite direction. By the time they were sorted out again, the entire variety troupe had gone green. Crowns askew, the Kings rushed to fight over the nearest spittoons, Tatty ran to the bar for a bottle of something to set her up against seasickness, and George Swaine probably disfigured his banjo permanently. The Harper girls took to their cabins and didn't emerge till the ship docked in New Orleans.

In Houston, after the short train ride from the coast at Galveston, they were greeted with another letter from Daddy. He said as how the winter had been earlier colder than usual. He'd almost been sent to his Maker, riding out after the remaining cows on their range, trying to rouse the poor dumb creatures to stand up and move around themselves, so's they wouldn't freeze to death right there on the ground. He'd come home from one foray hanging icicles from his chin and elbows. Mama had had to put him to bed against frostbite, then, being low on fuel, had gone off to hunt cow chips herself for the fire.

"Poor Mama," Julie said. "She's never before had to go out in winter after chips."

"And neither have you," responded Lily. "Usually I spend all fall collecting them and stacking 'em to dry in the stable."

A string of May's guitar spronged out of key as she sat fussing with it on her lap. "Don't act like you do all the work around the place single-handedly, Lily! April and I have been out in the cold plenty, too. In fact, all of us have paid our dues out there with Daddy during the cold times. Why, last winter it got so bad one day that I couldn't play the guitar for an entire week, my fingers were that blue!"

"I notice you ain't been singing that much lately, May, either. You just worrying about Barly not being in touch all this time, or has the stage taken it out of you?"

"Don't you mention Barly, Lily Harper. You who only thinks

a male is good for wrestling with!" A violent strum punctuated her remark.

"Lay off, May, unless you figure I should've stopped cold in that Baltimore bank and considered Frank McCoy for future husband material! I guess that's what most Easterners figure we deserve, anyhow." She stopped. "You think Barly might be getting cold feet on account of the stagecoach business after all? That maybe a man in his position oughtn't have a wife that—"

May banged down her guitar. "Lily Harper, don't you ever suggest—"

"Sisters, please," Julie pleaded. "We've only got another five days here in Houston, then we'll be on our way to San Antonio. Let us try to remain civil up to and including our final agreed voting time."

"Isn't it a bit precipitate referring to it as the final voting time, Julie? The results could go either way."

Julie glanced at March before returning to her embroidery. It was yet another new piece, this one reading **HOME IS WHERE THE HEART IS.** She appeared to be expanding her artistic talents with this effort. She'd actually sketched a tiny ranch house in the background. "That remains to be seen."

"It certainly does," added June with enthusiasm. "Especially if the new addition to our skit is well written. My, I wish I could have a chance at playing Lily's role. That will be the plum!"

Lily was scrunched into the corner of the latest settee in their latest boardinghouse room, her legs tucked under her. "I'd be delighted to hand it over, June, only that Colt weighs a ton and you couldn't even hold it steady."

"I could, too! A true actress can do anything she sets her mind to, Lily Harper!"

"Like Julie says, that remains to be seen. It surely does. Although why you're still so het up on spending your life on the stage beats me. This last couple of months should have got it out of your system good and proper. That goes for the rest of you, too, especially you, March. You're going to have to face up to Tom's being gone and getting on with the rest of your real life sooner or later."

Lily was rewarded with a glare and switched her attention to the sack of bananas and oranges on the floor that she'd bought on the levee in New Orleans as a treat for Mama. She'd been particular about the bananas, choosing the very greenest to be had. They'd been yellowing, and even beginning to brown from day to day. Lily wasn't at all sure the fruit would make it to the Double H. With that in mind, she pulled the sack over and carefully selected what seemed to be the ripest banana.

"I don't see how there could be any decision but one to anybody reasonable," she continued, peeling it slowly. "Anybody not stagestruck permanent, like June. Extra money seems to be like these bananas. It ripens fast, then just gets thrown away. Money got us into every single one of our messes, including this here dramatic tour. And educational as that's been, I'd throw it all away in a second if it could get us back to the time before Daddy's first scheme."

"Forget it, Lily," said March. "Daddy's been scheming since before you were born. He'll be happy to have us back, but none of it is going to change him any, and you know it."

Lily humphed and selected another ripe banana to present to Tatty. At least it was nice to have someone to complain to when she got done with one of these sessions with her sisters.

📖 They finally arrived in San Antonio at the tail end of January. If any of the Harper girls had been secretly wishing that there would be a welcoming party to meet them, like they'd hinted in their letters home once they knew their schedule, they were disappointed. Lily uncramped herself from the coach first, emerging into a fine, cold drizzle. "I hope the rooms Mr. Pastor set up for us here are near the Alamo. I always wanted to see the place, even if Granddaddy Winslow run out on it."

Her sisters were now rearranging themselves on the street as well, and a second stagecoach with the remainder of the troupe was pulling up behind.

"Didn't Mama say her old house was down along the river?" May was trying to remember. "Do you suppose our grandparents are still there?"

"If they're as die-hard set in their ways as Daddy says, they've got to be," Julie said. "Still and all, Lily, it certainly might be nice to meet them after all these years. Mama says my hand at stitching reminds her of her own mother's."

"What do you think?" April asked March.

"I think Daddy might not approve. It would be tantamount to sneaking behind his back, knowing his feelings on the subject. However, one ought to consider Mama's feelings on occasion, too. I'm sure *she* would dearly love to know how her parents are faring. We'd have to make the approach a suitable one, though."

"We'll send them a proper, formal note, and passes for the show!"

March spoke with admiration. "An excellent solution, June. It just might work . . ."

"Come along now, dearies, do you mean to stand out here in the weather till we all get galloping pneumonia?" Tatty was bearing down on them. "Do shake a leg, girls. Help is needed with these trunks."

The Harper girls composed a note to their grandparents that very night, and had it delivered by messenger boy the next morning. They'd enclosed passes for the show, hoping their grandparents would acknowledge the gift in the proper spirit and let them know when to expect them in the audience.

As it turned out, the elder Winslows did neither. They did, however, appear one evening in the middle of the week, as the girls discovered when they plunged into the usual stage-door crowd.

Smack in the middle of their admirers stood a very stern old couple. Lily would have marked them down as moralizers, or at least leaders of the local Temperance League, and would have ignored them completely, if she hadn't been struck by a remarkable resemblance between the woman and their own mother. The fact of the matter was that this woman had a remarkable resemblance to all five of her own sisters, too.

"Grandmama Winslow! And Granddaddy Winslow! You've got to be!"

In a moment her sisters were swarming around the older couple, equally excited. They stopped just short of actually touching or hugging them, though. Their stance was too formidable for that. Finally, Granddaddy spoke. "Well, Gertrude. What did I tell you. Just as common as you please, the lot of them."

"Please, Mr. Winslow, they are our only daughter's flesh and blood—"

"Too true, Gertrude, too true. This just proves we were correct to disown Gwendolyn as we did twenty years ago. We knew nothing good would come of her running off with that rowdy cowboy."

"You disowned her, Mr. Winslow, not—"

"Here's the result," Granddaddy continued, relentlessly. "All six of them disgracing themselves on the stage. As if their former sins weren't sufficient. Have you seen enough, Gertrude? Are you satisfied?"

Without another word, Granddaddy Winslow about-faced, pulling Grandmama after him into the night's gloom. Lily and her sisters were too shocked to stop them, or even speak up in their own defense. It was Tatty who came to their rescue.

"Well, I never, indeed. I heard the whole thing. Every word of it. Just you come on home with me, dearies, and Tatty will make you a nice hot cup of tea to give you comfort. Imagine anyone not being proud of each and every one of you! Why, if you were mine, I would've scratched out their righteous eyes. Maybe I will anyway!"

She actually began bustling off in their direction, but March pulled her back.

"It's no good, Tatty. Even our own flesh and blood won't speak to us. This is the end." March's words were filled with despair. "No Tom to stand up for me, nobody to meet us when we arrived back here practically home. No one to understand that we've long since redeemed ourselves, and have been working hard to save Daddy and his ranch. There's nowhere left for us."

Lily was sitting in Tatty's tiny room, watching their protector fiddle with a hand of solitaire. Tatty was humming "It's Better to Be an Old Man's Darling Than a Young Man's Slave." They'd just finished their last matinee, and tonight would be their final show. Maybe. Even now her sisters were waiting for Lily. Waiting to meet for the vote that would determine their futures.

"How would you sum up your life altogether, Tatty? I mean on the stage and all?"

Tatty turned over a card, then made several swift rearrangements in the vertical rows on the table before her. "For one thing, there's been too much time for solitaire, sweetie. Oh, I almost settled down to married bliss a few times, but something always went wrong at the last minute. Stage people just don't seem to be very good at that sort of thing. I would've maybe preferred a little cottage somewhere, with my own youngsters to feed and dress and raise. Truth to say, to stay in one place for that long, I would've settled for a shack. But it didn't seem to be set up for me in the great Stage Bill of Life. It seems to me sometimes that acting people are a lot like you Southerners—outcasts from the rest of the world." She focused on her face cards a moment, then looked up. "So I guess I'll just keep moving on, as long as somebody is willing to pay me to warble out at an audience. And as long as my voice can warble."

"Where will you go after that, Tatty?"

"Go? Well, I guess when I'm no good for that anymore, I'll stop somewhere long enough to die."

"Oh, Tatty! With nobody you love around? That's just not right! When you're ready to retire, you come out to the Double H and *I'll* take care of you!"

"You expect to be there, with your daddy still hanging on to the place that long, Lily? No matter how down I sound, I ain't planning on being kicked out, and kicking off, that soon!" Tatty rearranged a few more cards. "Hadn't you better be off to your sisters for the big meeting?"

"I don't want to go. March has got them all so low with her ideas about Eastern-style reputations that most everyone but Julie and me is scared of going back home. Even May. I'm real sorry now I ever mentioned anything to her about Barly maybe having second thoughts. She ought to know he ain't got room in his head for but one direct thought at a time . . . They've forgotten that in Texas, people got more open minds—leastways, people that ain't trying to act like warmed-over Easterners, like our grandparents. I'm afraid they'll vote for the road, and I'll be stuck with all of them forever and ever." Lily groaned with misery. "I swear, Tatty, the stage is starting to feel more like prison to me every day!"

" 'Stone walls do not a prison make / Nor iron bars a cage,' " Tatty quoted with a twinkle in her eye. "Maybe you ought to take up solitaire." Then she relented. "I hate to disillusion you, lovey, but *Young and Dangerous* ain't got but a few more months going for it, no matter what Tony Pastor says, and no matter how many more bank robberies you foil. You get through Chicago and back to New York and you'll find you're old news. And there ain't nothing as stale as old news."

Lily brightened. "That means we'd have to go home!" Then her face clouded once more. "But we'd probably be stranded in New York with not enough money to do it. April's the only one squeezing pennies for that ranch Rick wants. March has already used up most of her hope-chest money on bonnets and fripperies in New Orleans. And May went and spent yesterday in a music shop pricing parlor organs."

Tatty snorted. "How's she planning on lugging one of them around on the road?"

"I'm not sure, but knowing May, she'd find a way."

Tatty turned over a final card, then shoved them all together in a heap of frustration. "Lost again. That's usually the way with solitaire. I just don't know why I tax myself with it like I do." But her hands began to gather and shuffle the cards once more, and in a moment she was laying out a fresh game. "If I was you, I'd try to convince the sisters to hold off on the vote till you get back home to your ranch. You've got to go back anyways, at least for a visit. Don't burn your bridges before you have to."

Lily got up to go. "I was really looking forward to buying a new saddle for Checkers, now that I've got the money saved, from the reward and all, but if I won't be using it regular like . . ."

"For what it's worth, you tell your sisters that Tatty's been insulted more than once in her career. It wasn't by flesh and blood, because I haven't any of that left to my name, but it hurt just the same. The show went on nevertheless. You tell them to reach inside for some of that Harper spirit I saw in New York City and Baltimore!"

When Lily arrived back at the rooms, she found her sisters sitting around, waiting impatiently. March held a pile of paper slips in front of her.

"One thing we decided in your absence, Lily, was to take up Julie's suggestion and make this vote a secret one. That way we'll avoid unnecessary accusations after the fact. We'll each just write *home* or *stage* on our own piece of paper, fold it up, then throw it into my bonnet here."

There were a few quiet nods, and March began distributing the paper. But before they took turns with the one stubby pencil they owned, Lily made a last-ditch effort.

"I still don't see why we have to do this! Mama and Daddy will always be there, back at the ranch, to welcome us home. Whatever we do or done."

"It's not Daddy and Mama at issue here, Lily. You know that."

April and June had that same closed-up, obstinate look about them as March had. May, too.

"And Tatty says . . ." But Lily stopped. No amount of begging or protestation was going to help.

When it came to her turn, Lily took the pencil and stomped over to the settee. She laboriously spelled out *home* and studied her effort for a long moment, then marched back to the table to throw it into the waiting hat.

"That's all of us, then." March mixed the votes up with her

long, graceful fingers, and chose the first one to read aloud.

"Stage." She smoothed it out and placed it in front of her carefully, then reached for the second.

"Stage." It was placed precisely atop the first.

"Home."

Lily breathed a sigh of relief as that vote formed the beginnings of a second pile.

The fourth vote was also a *home*. Unfortunately, it was followed in quick succession by two more *stages*. March looked up.

"The decision seems to be to continue on the road. We'll send a telegram to Mr. Pastor in the morning."

Julie broke out into sobs, and Lily reached for her wrap and stalked out the door. There wasn't anything further to be said, and she didn't feel like sticking around playing at being a good loser. All the way out of the boardinghouse and down to the river, Lily's head was filled with visions of the Harper girls, aging slowly but surely into carbon copies of Tatty: hennaed hair and no place to call home.

Lily walked clear from the theater over to the crumbling Spanish mission that was the Alamo. She ignored the Northern soldiers of the occupation lounging around their barracks next door and paced alone through the high, open spaces with nothing but the sounds of scuffled rubble on the stone floor beneath her feet and a few winter birds flying in and out of the glassless windows. Brave men had died here: Jim Bowie, Davy Crockett, William Travis . . . They'd believed in something so hard that giving their lives had seemed worthwhile.

Lily stopped by a small, cell-like room opening off one side of the mission's nave. What did she believe in? Light was fading from the high windows. It could have been in this very room that Colonel Bowie had lain on his sickbed, rousing himself from his fever to give orders against Santa Anna.

The answer suddenly seemed very clear. Lily believed in Texas and the Double H Ranch, by heaven. She also believed the Harper girls had done enough penance for their mistakes. It was time to go home, no matter what the vote'd decided. But Lily didn't want to go home like this. She wanted to go home proud. As proud and sure of herself as these men had been about Texas.

Of a sudden, she spun around and set off in the direction of the river. She refused to surrender the fort.

A few hours later, Lily was perched atop a stool between her sisters, throwing some unneeded rouge on her cheeks.

"Going all out for our final night in San Antonio, Lily?"

"I wish it was our final night, period, June. I'm that fed up with all of it!" She stopped herself from adding, "and all of you, too." None of them seemed that entranced by their decision to continue the tour, either. None but June.

Lily glanced in the mirror a last time, gave her braid a shake, then put her elbows on the makeup ledge and her head in her hands. Thoughts of her impulsive visit that afternoon to her grandparents' richly appointed house—rich, but still empty and too cold, even with that fire in the library grate—swam through her head. She'd probably made a mistake throwing all her cards out on the table like that. They'd listened to her piece civilly, Grandmama acting like she just wanted to jump up and hug Lily forever, only holding back on account of Granddaddy and his stubbornness. Lily had finally walked out when it looked like it'd come to a standoff. More like run out, taking no heed of her grandmama's voice begging her to stop.

Visions of the Double H in the heat of summer swam up at Lily next. They'd had some good times together there, right enough, all of the Harpers. The cattle rustling had been funny, in a way, and building Daddy's still and plotting for the stagecoach robbery had brought all six sisters closer together than they'd ever been. In retrospect, all those mistakes seemed like a golden time. But recounting the last part of it—the actual stagecoach robbery—every night on the stage was just downright tawdry. Maybe Granddaddy and Grandmama Winslow were right about that. Maybe the lot of them were just common actresses and good for nothing more, like March said.

Lily didn't even notice the sharp knock at the door. It was March who shook her out of her thoughts, and spoke more gently than she had for too long. "It's time, Lily. Please pull yourself together. We're still the Harper Girls. It's our duty to do our best at whatever it is we're doing. That's the way it's always been."

Lily raised her head, wiped her eyes, and followed her sisters onstage for Scene One of *Young and Dangerous*.

As Tatty had floated down from her trapeze, and George Swaine had finished his "Dixie" banjo solo, the Harper girls were collecting their things from the dressing room. They did it quietly, listening to the final applause dying away out front. Finally, when there was nothing that could possibly delay them any further, they picked up their bags of makeup, slung their costumes over their arms, and trudged to the stage door.

"If Ned Brewster and his stagecoach are on schedule, we should be in Fredericksburg this time tomorrow night."

"That's so, May. Do you think Barly will look on us long enough to round up a wagon to get us to the Double H the next morning?"

"I'm sure I couldn't comment on that, Lily."

March shoved against the stage door, not wanting to hear any more. She glanced out apprehensively, like she'd done since the unexpected meeting with their grandparents, and pulled back instantly. The door slammed shut again and her bundled costumes fell to the floor. April dropped her own bundle, and her arms were around her sister in a moment.

"Whatever is the matter, March? You look like you've seen a ghost. Are you about to faint on us?"

"No, I . . . Do look outside for yourself, April. I can't stand it if it's only a dream!"

"What are you going on about?"

Lily dumped her own burdens, pushed past her oldest sisters, and stepped into the night.

There wasn't any top hat, and there weren't any flowers, but Tom Carter was waiting there just the same. He was in his old ranch clothes, from neckerchief and winter sheepskin coat on down to scruffy boots. And he was carrying two things. The first was a fine lady's sidesaddle. The second was a very small velvet box.

Lily turned around and shot her arm in the door. In a moment March was hovering close behind her, the rest of the girls staring over her shoulder.

"March, please. I beg you, talk to me! Forgive me!"

March looked like she would've forgiven Tom anything short of murder at that point.

With her usual flair for timing, Tatty picked this moment to trail out after them. "Is this young man disturbing any of you girls? Just give me the word and Tatty'll send him to kingdom come and back!"

Lily stopped her friend. "Just a minute, Tatty. Tom's maybe come to his senses. Give March a moment to find hers, too."

March did, and she and Tom were in each other's arms. When the commotion died down, Tatty handed Lily a letter. "This came for you just before you stormed in like you did for the show. I took the liberty of saving it for now."

Lily opened it under the gaslight, saw who it was from and felt her stomach drop. "It's for all of us from Grandmama and Granddaddy Winslow. They say they had a very interesting visit from me—I'll explain about that part later. They also say their feelings remain mixed, but if we'd be willing to meet at their house for dinner tomorrow, maybe the subject of all of us could be discussed in more appropriate surroundings."

Lily gave her flabbergasted sisters her biggest grin in a long, long time.

☞ With Tom's reappearance, and after the Harper girls had survived a slightly strained but still satisfactory peace dinner with their grandparents, their tarnished reputations didn't feel so tarnished and they sent a negative response to Tony Pastor. Lily figured he was going to be a disappointed man, especially since he'd gone all out on the new Baltimore bank holdup scene and had even written in another raise for them in the fresh contract he'd promised. George Swaine and the rest of the troupe philosophically packed up and headed East, but Tatty decided she needed a little vacation from the stage and moved into the Double H to help out with all the wedding preparations.

Daddy and Mama welcomed the lot of them with tears and bone-crushing hugs, and after supper their first night back, Daddy held a celebratory burning of the paid-up note from the bank in San Antonio, then followed that by burning the one from the Fredericksburg bank, which the girls had managed to repay in excess, leaving Daddy with a small nest egg. All of them cheered as the papers went up in smoke, symbolically closing that piece of their lives, but Lily estimated she wasn't the only Harper girl secretly holding her breath against Daddy's pulling a similar stunt anytime soon.

The wedding preparations went on for some time, seeing as how March chose to marry up with Tom Carter on her nineteenth birthday. Then there was April's wedding to arrange on *her* birthday. Nobody had ever doubted Rick's intentions for a moment, and he had been waiting for April with open arms—and freshly trimmed whiskers—when Barly and their caravan of buggies had pulled up to the Double H.

Barly himself had been haunting every stagecoach coming north through Fredericksburg for the entire month of January, according to Ned Brewster, who finally drove them all back from San Antonio. Lily had been afraid that Barly was going to squeeze May to death when he hauled her out of the coach, enfolded her, legs kicking, several feet above the ground, and refused to put her down. But May seemed to survive the mauling all right. Then she lit into him as to why he'd worried her so by not writing. Poor Barly just held up his huge fingers and said while they were good for lots of things, writing wasn't one of them.

So then, by the time they got to May's birthday wedding, the Harpers had gotten the ceremony down to a fine science. They'd managed to catch Judge Wiley while he was presiding locally for each and every one of the events. He acted amused, and possibly even honored to be adding the civic touches after the preacher officiated at the ceremonies in the ranch-house parlor. Ooh-long and his brand-new bride, Lotus Flower, helped with the catering. Lotus Flower was not a whole lot older than Lily herself, but she seemed entranced with her new husband. Also, she took to the Texas chile pepper right off, so it looked like another marriage made in heaven.

After April and Rick had been settled in for the interim in a tiny house at Izzy Henry's ranch, and March and Tom had gone off up to the north to settle the new lands he'd used his trust funds to buy, and May had blissfully moved her piano back to Fredericksburg and Barly's neat adobe house, Tatty declared she'd been rejuvenated, and was ready for the road again. With an excited June in tow, she headed back for New York City and bookings at Pastor's Opera House. Before they left, Lily decided that if the stage was what June truly wanted, she might as well have it. With that in mind, she hauled June up to Dead Man's Canyon for a lot of target practice with her new Colt, so that if June ever took on the role of Lily Harper, she'd be ready for it.

As for Julie, she hung every last one of her new mottoes around the ranch-house walls. Then she settled in on the veranda with her new line of stitchings—quilts and pillowcases—as if nothing would ever move her again, Mama rocking contentedly next to her. Granddaddy and Grandmama Winslow hadn't made it to the weddings, but they'd sent presents to each of the girls, and a letter to Mama which made her laugh, and then cry, before she tucked it away in her own hope chest.

Lily had watched everything settle down. When it seemed like there were no more surprises or events to deal with, she went out riding the range with Daddy one day, astride a Checkers resplendent in his San Antonio hand-tooled saddle and trappings.

Lily took in a deep breath of the spring air, filled as it was with everything she loved: juniper, sage, cow droppings.

"Those Longhorns are still wandering around free in the Big Thicket, Daddy."

"The thought has crossed my mind over the past few months,

181

daughter. In fact, it occurred to me I might have been a mite precipitate in casting away that opportunity, untried. And maybe I've been a mite uppity in not considering their strengths, too. Longhorn been surviving around here a lot longer than my purebred black Angus."

"You mean, you might just consider a little mixed breeding, Daddy?"

"Worse things have been suggested. You take the ability of the Longhorn to ignore the Texas Fever, along with its natural adjustment to extremes of temperature—"

"And add that to the meaty bulk of the Angus—"

"You got the idea, Lily."

"When do we head out for the Big Thicket, Daddy?"

"Would tomorrow be too soon?"

"Nope. It'd be just fine by me."